THE REAL WORLD,
AND THE OTHER REAL WORLD

/.\/\./\/.\/\

The Real World, and the Other Real World

SHORT FICTION

by Marcia Lewton

/.\./\.\/\.\./\.\/.\/\.\./\.\./\.\./\.\/\.\./\.\/\.\./\.\/\

Printed in Victoria, Canada

National Library of Canada Cataloguing in Publication

Lewton, Marcia
     The real world, and the other real world / Marcia Lewton.
ISBN 1-4120-0987-1
    I. Title.
PS3612.E87R43 2004   813'.6   C2003-904304-5

Composition of this work was supported in part by a grant from the IndianaArts Commission. Thanks go also to the Ragdale Foundation and the Virginia Center for the Creative Arts for their support. Earlier versions of some of these stories have appeared in the following periodicals: InPrint, The Minnesota Review, Indiana Review, Quarry I, New Fiction From Indiana, Ms., Indi/Annual, Iowa Woman, Thema, and The Flying Island. All were published under the name Marcia Blumenthal. "Tearing" also appeared in the short story collection Bitches and Sad Ladies, edited by Patricia Rotter, published by Harpes Magazine Press, and as a skit on The Richard Pryor Show. Photograph of the author by Matthew Gatheringwater. Cover art by author, photographed by Eric McRea. Book design and compositon by Valerie Brewster, Scribe Typohraphy.

TRAFFORD

This book was published *on-demand* in cooperation with Trafford Publishing.
On-demand publishing is a unique process and service of making a book available for retail sale to the public taking advantage of on-demand manufacturing and Internet marketing. **On-demand publishing** includes promotions, retail sales, manufacturing, order fulfilment, accounting and collecting royalties on behalf of the author.

Suite 6E, 2333 Government St., Victoria, B.C. V8T 4P4, CANADA

Phone	250-383-6864	Toll-free	1-888-232-4444 (Canada & US)
Fax	250-383-6804	E-mail	sales@trafford.com
Web site	www.trafford.com	TRAFFORD PUBLISHING IS A DIVISION OF TRAFFORD HOLDINGS LTD.
Trafford Catalogue #03-1356		www.trafford.com/robots/03-1356.html

10   9   8   7   6   5   4   3   2

For my daughters,
Ginger Monka & Jill Blumenthal

/\/\/\/\/\

/\\/\\/\\/\\/\\

Contents

THE REAL WORLD,
AND THE OTHER REAL WORLD

.\\.\\.\\.\\

Duke Drunk in the Driveway

If there was trash in her family, my mama knew where it was, and although she never told me outright, I knew where it was too.

This was surprising, since none of her people did the things she pointed out as *looking* trashy: smoking on the street, letting a sweat-stained bra show at the armpits of a sleeveless dress. Wearing lipstick so thick it smeared off on the rim of a glass, or a skirt that rode up over your knees when you sat, or high-heeled shoes with ankle straps. Having peroxided hair that hung down in a big brassy fluff.

Mama's sisters agreed. They would get together on Saturdays at Hallie's house and sit around their cups of tan coffee and talk about people. My father didn't go to the Saturday gatherings; this was during the war and he was working six days a week at the plant. My cousins and I would listen to the sisters run people down for a while, then go play outside, and when we came back, they would still be talking.

The question of trash in Mama's family, however, had nothing to do with being trashy-looking. It had to do with things like divorces and mortgages and, as I learned much later, affairs and abortions. On a lesser level it had to do with having a husband who got drunk and carried on. It had to do with leaving food out on the table for the flies to walk on, and keeping one glass at the sink for everyone to drink out of, and having too many dogs.

Bringing my knowledge of this to consciousness took putting two and two together. Mama had always told me that my father thought her people were trashy. "Just because we like to laugh and sing and we don't walk around with nails between our teeth," she said. But I figured out that it wasn't the laughing and singing she was worried about; it was those other things, the things she told me not to tell. "Don't tell Daddy," she would say, if there was talk about hard luck with money at Hallie's on Saturday. Or "Don't say anything about what happened," if Hallie's husband Duke was loafing around in his undershirt drunk as a skunk. I knew that the things I wasn't supposed to mention were the evidences of real trash, and being trashy-looking was different.

Being trashy-looking was different from being ugly-looking too. If you looked trashy, all you had to do was change your ways, but if you were ugly-looking, you'd better shoot yourself. That was what the sisters said. If we were out on the porch and someone went by that they thought was ugly-looking, one of them would say, "If I looked like that, I'd shoot myself, wouldn't you?"

I thought about that a lot, growing up, checking mirrors.

One of Mama's sisters was ugly-looking, with a face like a Pekinese and brown, crooked teeth. That was Aunt Hallie. She was not willing to shoot herself, however. She compromised and said that when she died, she would have herself cremated. "I don't want people lining up at the casket looking in at my ol' ugly face," she said.

But even that compromise was called into question when Hallie got liver cancer and thought she might have to follow through.

She was put in the hospital on the day she was supposed to be in court to get divorced a second time from Duke, whose big trashy flaw was being drunk out in the driveway and too fat for Hallie to drag indoors. So there he lay in the driveway, and although he had always been in the house or on the porch when I was there, I pictured this driveway business as a now-permanent state. Hallie probably had to take his meals out to him and a change of undershirts now and then, and of course she had to get him another bottle when he hollered.

They had been divorced for a while before, but then Duke went on the wagon to show Hallie how crazy he was about her, and they got remarried. The remarriage was even trashier than the first divorce had been. I wasn't supposed to tell Daddy about it, and of course I wasn't to mention the second divorce either.

I knew about it though. I listened to my mama and her sisters gossip, both at their Saturdays and on the phone, when I would make myself comfortable in the kneehole of the desk while Mama talked from the armchair alongside.

"Hallie's nuts," I had heard Mama say to her oldest sister Olive when the news came that Hallie and Duke were back together. Mama's feet were set flat on the floor as she delivered her opinion. "He's got her convinced that he loves her enough to stay on the wagon, but you and I know that love never means much to a drunk, compared to the bottle."

The news that Hallie's second divorce was being put off because of the hospital trip came by phone too, and then the news that her tests showed a liver cancer that had spread around something terrible before Hallie went to the doctor. She had thought it was life with Duke and the smell of Four Roses that was making her feel so sick.

Mama went to the hospital to visit. The weather was bad, with a heavy spring rain, and my father and I drove her there and sat in the car while she saw Hallie. When she came out, she told us that Hallie's eyes had turned yellow. She wanted to go and visit again the next night, but Daddy said once was enough, and she was afraid to take the streetcar clear across town alone at night.

A few days later a call came from Hallie at the hospital. I settled myself in the kneehole to listen. There was a ragged spot in the rug down under the desk. I unraveled it while I listened, pulling threads that went clear out to the edge of the rug and back.

"Of course I still have it," said Mama. She rummaged through the desk and brought out the folder full of old Christmas cards where she hid important papers from my father. "And of course you can use it if you need to, but you're not going to need to. They can do more than you think they can, Hallie."

But Mama didn't believe what she was saying. As soon as she hung up, she called Olive.

"Hallie's afraid Duke's going to bury her in the double grave they bought when they went back together," Mama told Olive. "She wants me to sell her that cemetery lot of mine."

My mama had bought a lot of her own in the Mt. Pleasant Cemetery where all her people were buried. There had been an awful fight when my father found out. He had been so mad he started to tear up the deed and Mama had to snatch it away and hide it.

"We've got a cemetery lot," he yelled. "I shelled out good money for it!"

"Yes," she answered, "in that stuck-up cemetery with your stuck-up relatives."

"You promised forever!"

"Forever only means while I'm alive," she said. "I promised till death do us part. After I'm dead I'm going to be with my people."

But Hallie could have the lot, she said now. "She needs it worse than I do."

Mama cried, talking to Olive. "She hasn't got a chance, has she?" Then there was something from Olive and Mama said, "At least she can rest easy now, though, knowing she'll be there with us instead of depending on Duke to sober up enough to put a few flowers on her grave now and then."

Mama told Daddy that Hallie was going to use her cemetery lot, but she didn't tell him that it was to avoid Duke, because, of course, Daddy thought that Duke had been out of the picture since the first divorce. Daddy just nodded, didn't even ask if Hallie was going to cough up the money to pay for it.

The cancer ate away at Hallie's liver, and after another couple of weeks of bad weather, the word came that she probably wouldn't live through the night. My father took Mama to see her again, and he made her a nice hot cup of coffee when we all got home. He even brought her slippers downstairs. Her shoes were wet from the rain and her face all messed up from crying. "She wasn't my favorite sister," she said, already using the past tense, "but she used to beat up the older kids that picked on me."

Just then the phone rang. My father started to answer it, but Mama said, "It's probably for me," and picked it up. "Hello," she said. As she listened to the caller her face stiffened into disapproval, and when she started talking, her voice took on that tone that didn't want to be associated with trash. My father stood there waiting. Finally Mama shook her head at him, covered the mouthpiece and whispered, "It's not about Hallie. It's just Olive." My father left her alone then and went in the living room to read the paper. I stayed, of course, and curled into the kneehole, picking the rug.

"If he's drunk, he won't listen to me either," said Mama.

She had to be talking about Duke, I thought. I pictured him fat and drunk lying in the driveway behind his old blue Chevrolet, the gravel making dimples in his pink flesh.

"The nerve of him! You'd have thought they'd keep him out. Couldn't she even have her last day in peace?"

Oh? Maybe Duke had gotten himself out of the driveway after all and gone to see Hallie. It appealed to me, him sobering up enough to visit his dying wife, a reconciliation. I wasn't as anti-Duke as Mama was. He always had a good, smelly bathroom joke to tell us kids.

"Hallie never mentioned that he'd been there," said Mama. "But then she was too sick to say more than a word or two."

"Well, I'll give it a try," she told Olive, finally. "But I don't think he's going to stay away just because I ask him to."

After hanging up from Olive, she gave the operator Hallie and Duke's number. She waited and waited while it rang. Finally she tensed. "Duke? I thought you were never going to answer that phone." I could see her one leg crossed over the other and her foot twitch back and forth as she listened to him. "Oh come on now, Duke, you know you don't want to do that." I got hold of a promising piece of rug yarn and pulled. This conversation made no sense. "Well, how're you planning on doing it?" she asked. A pause. Then, "They say it takes a long time and isn't very pleasant."

I found out what was going on when she called Olive back. She talked low so my father wouldn't hear. "He says he's going to kill himself," she said. "He says Hallie's a-laying up there dying and he doesn't want to go on living without her. I tried to kid him out of it, ask him how he was going to do it and all, you know, to get him to talk instead of doing anything. He said he was going to drown himself. My call got him out of the bathtub. Olive, he's drunk as a skunk." Her voice was completely disgusted. "Lord only knows what he'll think up next."

Then Olive talked a while and Mama said, "I suppose it's a good idea, but you'd better do the calling. They might show up here in a squad car to ask questions and Clark would have a fit."

Mama hung up just as I had another piece of yarn running out to the edge. "Gwennie! You're tearing that rug right out from under me," she said. "Why aren't you in bed?"

Olive, of course, sent the police out to check on Duke. They found him back in the bathtub with the hot water running in on him. He wasn't drowned, but he was scalded. They got an ambulance to take him to the hospital.

And while all this was happening, Hallie died. When I found out about it the next day, I pictured dead Hallie escaping out the back of the hospital in a hearse while naked Duke roared up in front in an ambulance.

At the funeral home on Saturday Duke was the topic of conversation, not Hallie. Olive had gone over after she called the police and found them having a hard time with him. He was in the tub hollering, "Hallie's a-dying and I want to die with her. I ain't done nothing criminal. You got no right to barge in here." They had to haul him out, though he wasn't able to put up much of a fight, being both drunk and burned.

My cousin Joe crooked his finger for me to come behind the flowers where he whispered that Duke's skin had come off. "Slipped right off when they picked him up," Joe said. "Same thing as when you scald a tomato. They draped his skin over the shower curtain rod like a suit and left it hanging there."

I'd heard enough about Duke. I stayed away from Joe and hung by my mama. She was dressed up in her blue spring suit with her hair curled fresh from the beauty parlor. My father had offered to show up at the funeral home after work, but she told him she might have to stay all evening. "I'll call when we're ready to leave and you can come pick us up." The last thing she wanted was him there taking it all in.

Hallie in the casket was dressed up too. She hadn't had herself cremated after all. Her eyes were closed, so I couldn't see the yellow. Her mouth had been sewed up in a tight little circle of gathers. But she didn't look so ugly. There are lots worse dogs than Pekinese.

Mama waited until everyone else had left before she called my father. He came right away, wearing his suit, and instead of honking for us, he came inside and signed the book.

From the way Mama described the day as we rode home, I didn't recognize it. She made no mention of Duke, and she gave me a good hard poke when I asked if you could peel a person in hot water like you did a tomato.

Duke died that night. I was still asleep when the call came the next morning, so all I knew was that the burns were too bad for them to save him. "Don't say anything," Mama warned me. "Daddy doesn't have to know anything about Duke." Her voice was gritty and she looked tired.

But she hid her weariness from Daddy when she pointed out how nice it was that the weather had changed. "It's been a long time since we had a mess of blue gills."

She was laying it on thick, but he fell for it. My father was happy-looking when he thought about fishing. But then the twinkle left his eyes. "I ought to show up out there this afternoon."

"Well, Clark," she answered, "you were there last night. Nobody's going to hold it against you that you didn't want to spend your one day a week with us hens."

His eyes cheered up again and he growled, "Not a chance of catching anything. Water's too high," which meant that he'd go to the lake anyway and put a line in.

Mama and I spent Sunday afternoon and evening just as we had Saturday, being at the funeral home all dressed up, though the atmosphere was rowdier, with more laughing and less whispering, and the grownups were not so strict about what we could do. We ate a lot of doughnuts and drank a lot of Cokes, and we played puddle tag in the parking lot. The room where Duke was going to be was closed. His calling hours didn't start until evening. We wondered if we'd get sick looking at him, and Joe told us that they couldn't embalm him if he didn't have skin to hold the fluid in. I felt queasy, but I wasn't going to let go of a chance to see a person without any skin.

Some people from Duke's family came to our parlor and talked to Olive, who was the oldest of the sisters and the boss of Mama's people. They called Mama into the conversation and all of them went in the director's office and closed the door.

Mama was frowning when they came out. "I'm the one she asked," she said. "It's terrible to refuse your own sister her dying wish."

But Olive was the boss. "You gave her wish while it mattered," she said. "She's gone now. Besides, she did love Duke when he wasn't drunk. And once he's down there in the ground, there's no way he's going to lay hands on a bottle." Olive was tall, wearing a hat with a wide brim and a dress with big shoulder pads.

So Mama put the deed back in her purse and went on being gracious with callers.

In the evening, when Duke's parlor was opened, I went in to look. There he was with his hair in little bristles just like always. I had never seen him wearing anything but an undershirt hanging out over his trousers, but now he had on a coat and tie. He still had skin, at least on his face, which was the only part that showed. The bottom of the casket was closed and instead of a blanket of flowers there was a flag folded into a thick three-cornered bundle lying on it. That meant he had been in the First World War, they said, like my father.

"See," I told Joe. "His skin didn't either come off."

"You just can't see because of the suit," answered Joe. "The skin didn't come off his face because he didn't put his face in the water."

"If he was trying to drown himself, he would have had to put his face in."

"Well, he didn't drown, did he?"

Maybe Duke had been too drunk to remember that you had to put your face in if you wanted to drown.

When everyone left that evening, Mama and I waited outside for Daddy to pick us up. She was quiet in the car and of course I had been coached to say nothing about Duke.

But the next morning when I got up, Daddy hadn't gone to work. It was a dark day, raining again. Mama looked all sallow-faced and straggly-haired. My father was going to the funeral. "It's in the union contract," he said. "Your wife's sister is immediate family."

Mama pressed his suit. She curled her hair and mine, too, with the curling iron. She was so tense that all I did when she got too close to my ear was give a little moan.

In the car the only noise was the windshield wipers thump-thumping across the glass. Mama wasn't talking. Duke's funeral wouldn't be until tomorrow. Mama's people were not very talkative with my father. Maybe there was still a chance he wouldn't find out anything.

Part way there, Mama asked Daddy to stop at a drugstore so that she could buy some aspirin for her headache. She stayed in the store a long time, and we arrived too late to visit with people before the service.

Nobody was laughing or acting rowdy at the funeral home today. People sat in rows of hard chairs instead of on soft couches around the room. We were family, so we sat in a little room with my aunts and uncles and cousins off to the side where the people who weren't family couldn't see us. An old woman wearing a lot of rouge played the organ. The minister spoke about Hallie as a good wife and a good woman, and he talked about the time that comes to all of us when we go to meet our Maker. I started crying then. It could have been Mama who died, I realized, and some day it would be. It was hard to stop crying, and I wished I had a hanky, but finally the funeral was over and we all filed out a back door to the parking lot where the cars were lined up for the drive to the cemetery. We waited, all three of us in the front seat.

After a while my father said, "What the hell's holding things up?"

"How would I know?" answered Mama.

We waited some more. I was getting hungry. We watched it rain, and we watched people getting in and out of their cars.

Finally the funeral director came out with his big black umbrella. He stopped at Olive's car, which was in front of ours, and talked in the window for a minute. He unstuck the little purple flag from the left front fender of her car and came on to us.

My father rolled down the window. "What's the story?" he asked.

The funeral director tugged at our flag. The magnet came unstuck. "The water level's too high to dig," he said. "They couldn't get down deep enough." His voice tried to be comforting. "We're going to have to wait." He wound the cloth around the little flag pole. "The other funeral's tomorrow. Maybe it'll dry up by then. We'll bury them both together." Then he went on to the next car.

"What's that numskull talking about?" Daddy growled.

Olive's family in the car ahead pulled up and turned around. They came back beside us. Olive called to Mama, "I'll talk to you later."

Mama nodded yes and then said to Daddy, "He's talking about Duke. Let's get out of here."

The car bucked; then Daddy steered out onto the street. "What about Duke?"

Mama's gloved fingers were laced tightly in her lap. "Hallie and Duke got remarried a year or so ago and bought a grave site together. Hallie's going to be buried there. That's why she's not being buried in the grave near the family."

Daddy drove on. He nodded. The windshield wipers went ka-thunk/swish, ka-thunk/swish. Then he said, "You're not making sense."

"Duke's dead too," said Mama. She took off her left glove and wadded it up.

"Duke's dead too," he echoed. A block later he asked, "What'd Duke die of, liver cancer?"

"He died of burns," she answered, with dignity. "He killed himself because he couldn't stand to go on living without her." Mama's other glove was off now. She gave both of them to me to hold as though she needed her hands free.

My father kept on nodding and driving. Finally he said, "How come the switch?"

She tried to act as though she didn't know what he was talking about. I sat small and quiet between them.

"All that mumbo-jumbo about using the other grave."

"Hallie was trying to get divorced when she got sick," said Mama reluctantly. "You know what a drunk he was." Her voice went faster. "Hallie had all she could stand of it. And when she found out she was going to die, she wanted to be buried with her own people."

My father's voice was peculiar when he finally spoke. "But he won, didn't he?" Just then a drop of water came from somewhere and landed on one of his coat buttons. "The poor son-of-a-bitch had to kill himself to do it, but he won."

I held my breath. I had never heard my father say "son-of-a-bitch" before. It was one of the things that my mother's trashy relatives said that I wasn't supposed to notice. I slid a glance at him, and just then another drop of water hit his button. He said it again, "The poor son-of-a-bitch."

When we got home, Mama made me go to school for the afternoon, and later on, the next time we got together with Olive, she gave the deed to the cemetery lot to her, as oldest and boss. The next person in the family to die without one could use it, she said. "If Clark feels that strongly," she said. And besides, she knew that Olive would give it back if it ever became necessary.

Ephesus, NJ

Every morning in the breakfast room Penny watches the three older of her four little boys and wonders if her husband Clifford's grip on them is going to hold for another day.

"Hang on to your chairs, boys," Clifford says, "until we've thanked the Lord for the new day and the food we're about to receive." He takes his place at the table.

The baby, of course, is exempt, but Matthew, David and Paul, none of them six yet, sit perfectly still for an amazing moment and hold the edges of their chairs while waiting for their father to choose who will say grace. Penny is torn between wanting to preserve the peace and hoping one of them will rebel.

Today Matthew is chosen. He begins to stammer, "We th-th-thank Thee, Lord," very slowly in a gruff, little-boy voice.

Penny's head is bowed for Clifford's sake, but she has decided not to thank the Lord ahead of time. She will wait and see. Maybe the new day will bring something.

Clifford has already run his four miles, showered and shaved. He is dressed to go into Atlantic City where he and his father scrape and drill the valuable teeth of wealthy patients.

Penny does not run. She is only twenty-four, ten years younger than Clifford, and keeping in shape is not a concern. "In shape for what?" she often wonders.

"Just a little way," Clifford sometimes urges her. "It would be good for the boys, too. That's the way a person gets the regime started." Other times he reminds her that the body is God's temple. "And if something ever happens, people will need to be in top physical condition if they're going to survive."

But she couldn't run with him anyway; she must set the table, slice the bananas and oranges, put out the granola and soy milk, and besides, getting the children out for a run first thing in the morning is not at all the way she wants to start the day. She has noticed that he himself runs without them.

This morning her slim body is enveloped in a loose Mother Hubbard. Her ponytail hangs to the front because of her bowed head. Her feet under the table are bare, but her slippers are well within reach, for Clifford hates the sight of bare feet.

He says he's afraid there are sharp things, pins or tacks, lost in the carpet, but Penny thinks there's more to it than that. He confessed to her when they were first married that when he was a dentistry student, his feet had been gang-raped by a group of girls at a party. They had held him down while two of them took off his shoes and socks and sucked his toes. "My feet hadn't been washed since morning," he said, "but that didn't bother them." He wondered later if toe-sucking was something he was supposed to do, or want done to him, if it was something everybody did and he just hadn't heard about it. Penny's first reaction was to be sympathetic over the violation of his body, but later the story got funnier as she thought about it, especially happening to someone like Clifford, whose toes are part of God's temple.

Matthew has become stuck on the word "food." The room is silent around him as he struggles, and Penny's own lips form the word and try to send it to him like a kiss. Finally he gets it out and goes on.

Penny is not thanking God for the granola any more than she is thanking Him for the new day. She believes that He can read her thoughts and knows she would rather have a bologna sandwich on soft white bread spread with Miracle Whip, the breakfast she used to fix for herself after her mother left early for work.

She realizes, however, that if she were to bring any of these foods into the house, Clifford would speak to her about it – in a nice way, of course, for Clifford goes out of his way to be nice. "The boys won't learn nutrition and lead a wholesome life unless we set the right example," he would urge. It is better for her to anticipate and avoid this speech than to actually hear it. It's hard to argue against nutrition and wholesomeness.

When the "Amen" is over and Matthew and his brothers may begin eating, Penny's feet ease into their slippers. She goes to the other end of the table, picks up the remote control, and switches on the TV, which is recessed in the breakfast room wall nearest Clifford. It is now 6:30, time for PBS *Morning College.* Penny takes all the PBS courses, no matter what they are: *English Literature, Becoming Computer Literate, Music History, Contemporary American Poets,* to name a few. She is convinced that each thing she learns becomes a pinpoint of light in her brain and that some day the pinpoints will connect and her whole mind will light up.

Ancient Greek Philosophy is the course that's running now; this morning's lecture is about Heraclitus. Penny looks past Clifford's strong, granola-chewing jaws to the baked remains of the Greek seaport of Ephesus, recently uncovered by archeologists. A Greek folk tune introduces the show.

"Heraclitus was descended from the kings of this city," says the instructor, "but he renounced the kingship and went into the hills where he subsisted on grasses and herbs, scorning his fellow men."

David, the second-born, is telling a long story in a lisp understood only by the family while Paul, the two-year old, giggles. Penny sees and hears them but is not impinged upon. She has heard the story before. David's lisp worries her — as does Matthew's stammer — and she is glad to be drawn away from it and the rest of the breakfast clamor into the program. She eats absently and gives an occasional bite of banana to the baby, who is banging the high chair tray with a plastic clown.

"When Heraclitus was invited by the king of Persia to reside at court, he refused. 'I have a horror of splendor,' he said, 'and cannot come to Persia, being content with little, when that little is to my mind.'"

Penny stares into space, transported by the picture past her family's wholesome splendor into the dry hills overlooking the Aegean. There she walks with a Heraclitus who looks like Zorba the Greek.

As the instructor talks she feels dust between her toes (which are bare again) and a hot wind in her face; her mouth is filled with the taste of olives.

Heraclitus, also barefoot beside her, utters remarkable statements: "All things are fair and good and right to God; but men think of some as wrong and others as right."

Penny wants to break into the program and agree, to say that bologna and granola are all the same to God, but Clifford is the one who would hear her, not Heraclitus.

"Fire was the key element for Heraclitus," says the instructor, "and things come into being by a conflict of opposites. Neither God nor man can shape them."

At the mention of God's limitations Penny glances quickly at Clifford. Clifford just as quickly leans to the TV and snaps it off. "Little pitchers," he says.

But before he finishes speaking, Penny is out of her chair and into the family room where she drops to the floor in front of the TV there.

The program resumes with a cool PBS voice: "Strife is the creative force, Peace the destructive. Fire turns into moisture, which condenses into water. Water congeals and turns into earth, being the downward path."

The TV picture is showing a diagram with licking flames, water droplets and a plowed field, all connected with little arrows, like a weatherman's chart. Suddenly one of the pinpoints in Penny's mind lights up and casts a cozy glow. She knows what's familiar about all this: Gerard Manley Hopkins' Heraclitean fire from *English Literature*. "Cloud-puffball, torn tufts, tossed pillows flaunt forth...." She has memorized the first few lines and recalls the ending, about the comfort of the Resurrection.

The instructor has the tone now of bring the lesson to a close. "Heraclitus did not suffer fools easily. It was to avoid their company that he renounced luxuries and went to live simply in the hills."

The Greek music comes on, and Penny feels something in her hair. Turning, she sees Clifford holding the baby down to her and feels the sharp, tangling tugs that the baby's fingers inflict on her hair. The thought passes through her mind as she takes the baby: I'll bet

Heraclitus didn't have four little boys to raise.

"I have an early appointment," says Clifford in a voice toneless with duty.

She stares at him. It occurs to her that all four boys look just like him. This is not really news, of course, yet at this moment it strikes her as forcefully as a headline. Her entire adult life has been spent as a vessel for the perpetuation of Clifford's genes.

"Here," he says, "I have to leave now. You'll be wanting these." And he takes her slippers from under his arm and puts them down beside her.

She ignores the slippers and cuddles the baby automatically while still staring up at Clifford's pale blue eyes fringed with white lashes and his wide mouth with the short upper lip that never quite seems to close – these features handed down four times already – the visible teeth making the mouth appear to be smiling even when it's not. It is always restful for her to be out of sight of that mouth, for it demands a perpetual smile in return.

The Greek music is still coming from the TV set, enticing her easily. She is not ready to come back to the real world. "When I was in school," she says dreamily, "we had only one lamp and it had a forty-watt bulb in it, and that was where I did my homework every night." The memory gives her an instant of comfort.

Clifford squats down to kiss the top of the baby's head, then hers. "Things will be easier for the boys. You must be thankful for that."

"Clifford, you sound...." She stops short. How can she scream at a husband who has just kissed her? She has almost said the thing that comes to her mind so often, the Clifford sounds like a recorded message. She wants to be careful not to blurt it out. She believes that the things people say to each other hang in the air forever. But he does, she thinks, whether she says it or not. His voice changes and she can almost see his hand turn a knob in his chest before he goes somewhere else while the message plays. She wonders where he goes; she has tried to find out, but all she gets is the recorded message saying, "Don't be foolish, Penny. I'm right here."

"I hope you didn't miss your program." He stands up now and starts across the room. "I was abrupt, I know, but you were sitting too far away to turn it off as quickly as I could."

She is puzzled. Is he saying that she would have turned off *Morning College?*

"You and I know that most of what you hear on TV isn't true, but we do have to be careful about the boys."

She disentangles the baby's fingers from the tendrils around her face.

"Have a nice day," he says, looking down at her. "Take some time off while Mother's here. It'll do you good to get out of the house."

What would happen if she said, "Stop talking like a SMILE pin?" It flashes through her mind, followed by Clifford's amazement, his treating her as though she were a disturbed person, her attempt to act unnaturally sane.

She nods, and keeps on nodding as he starts the car outside for the long drive into the city. The nodding relieves the tightness in her neck. The baby mirrors her movement, and they nod to each other until they are both laughing.

Penny knows Clifford doesn't really like commuting, though he never complains; that would be failing to accept God's will. He had hoped once to be a missionary dentist, but he gave it up, first when his father had a heart attack and needed help with the practice, then for good when Matthew was born. His life in the cavities can't be all that satisfying, she tells herself. He makes sacrifices for the family. But if that's true, why won't he speak out – and let her speak out – and abandon the continual smile that makes her face ache with good fortune?

Of course she will take time off, and gladly. She always goes out on Wednesday when Clifford's mother comes to give the children lunch and spend a few hours with them. Mrs. Zellen calls it "Grandma's Day" and laughs in a blonde, bouffant way over being a grandmother. Penny knows she's lucky to have a helpful mother-in-law who doesn't make trouble, lucky to have some relief from the boys. Not every woman has free time each week.

Wednesday is also the day she likes to call her own mother back home in Kokomo. It is her mother's morning off from the doctor's office where she has a job as a receptionist, and Penny calls early as prearranged.

Her mother picks up the phone on the first ring and wants to know right away what room Penny is in.

"I'm in the bedroom in the rocking chair with the baby." As she speaks, she sees herself in the mirror and sees the room through her mother's eyes, noting the thick, smoky-rose colored carpet, the paintings, the one whole wall of drawers and doors where everything can be kept separate instead of jumbled in a bureau.

"What about the big boys?"

Penny reassures her mother that she can see – and hear – them out the window riding their noisy vehicles around the asphalt track just inside the fence that circles the play area Clifford has made for them. She tells her mother the things about the children that she has saved up all week; her mother never tires of hearing about the boys.

"I know you'd tell me if he had...." Her mother hesitates. "But has Paul said any more words since last week?"

"No, Mother, I'll tell you when he does. They say his hearing is okay, he's perfectly normal, just a late talker. Don't worry." With this, Penny changes the subject. "Mother, how come we never went to church?" She feels nosy asking, as though it is a question her mother might not like.

"After we left your father, there wasn't time," is the answer. "By the time I worked two jobs, cooked the meals and did the housework, I didn't have time left over for anything else."

"Do you go now?"

"No. I guess I didn't form the habit when I was young enough, and now I like my Sundays the way they are. Why?"

"Clifford turned off my TV class in the middle of it this morning, and I couldn't tell him how rude he was because he was doing it for God."

"I can't imagine Clifford being rude."

"It isn't called being rude if God's on your side. Mother, he's even more religious than you realize. He prays all the time, he even kneels by the bed at night and wants me to kneel with him. Then when he gets in bed it's like having God in there too. You can't imagine. And since I don't come from any religion of my own, he just assumes I fall right in with his. He even says that's why he married me. That I was young and a *tabula rasa* and he could mold me. He pretends to be kidding, but I know he means it."

After this outburst there is a long silence.

"Well, Penny, I don't know what to say. It just seems to me that you're very well off. It's not every woman's got what you've got. And young as you are, too. Clifford's a good man." Then Penny's mother clears her throat significantly. "The rest of the plant closed down," she says.

"Oh no." Penny knows exactly what her mother means.

"And him with the family, and that house to pay for." She is talking about the high school sweetheart Penny didn't marry.

"Maybe he'll find something."

"Without any school? I tell you, Penny, you're well off that you didn't put your hopes there. You had enough years with nothing to know what it's like."

"I know, Mother. I just need a chance to think my own thoughts."

"Nobody can stop you."

"I need to declare what I think once in a while too."

Her mother laughs. "As long as you do your declaring in the basement with the washer and the dryer both running, you're probably safe."

This is no joke, for Clifford broke off with his sister Betty after the argument over whether God was dead or whether He was alive and well and still in charge.

"You can always talk to me," her mother says. "You know Clifford would never criticize you on account of the phone bill."

"I know." She wishes her mother would stop telling her how wonderful Clifford is.

Her mother gives a self-conscious little laugh. "I have a bit of news to tell you," she says. "I've got a date next weekend. I'm going to the Strawberry Festival in Indianapolis."

"Neat!" says Penny. "Who with?" This is real news. Her mother hasn't had a date in years.

"With one of Dr. Thom's patients. He's got an artificial hand. He was funny inviting me out, apologizing for the hand; it gave me a chance to tell him right off about my artificial breast. 'Well,' he says, 'they can keep each other busy, then, can't they?' It's such a comfort, Penny, having that out in the open and accepted."

"It must be." Penny feels a little envious. She will have to absorb the idea of her mother in a sexual situation, but for now she tells her to have a good time. "Wear the knit-string suit," she says. It is the color of juniper berries and looks good on her mother. "Watch out for that other hand."

Her mother's laugh sounds younger already. "There's a dance in the old dame yet," she says.

"You're not exactly old, Mother."

"No," says her mother, "I'm not, am I? I wasn't even twenty when you were born."

The conversation winds down and Penny hangs up and calls the boys inside to get them ready for Grandma's arrival. She enjoys this, the physical care of the children. Although in appearance these are Clifford's sons, in their wiggle and heft they belong to her. When Mrs. Zellen arrives, all their fingernails have been trimmed, their ears cleaned and their clothes taken off and put back on straight for Grandma.

"Would you kindly mail these for me if you're going through town?" Mrs. Zellen asks this first thing coming in the door. "I drove right by the post office and forgot them."

Penny nods and accepts the bundle of postcards. She knows what they are. One of her mother-in-law's good works is to send a postcard with the message, "Jesus loves you," to everyone she meets or hears of. A postcard is something tangible, something the recipient can keep, not just a message. In summer she writes them while working on her tan at the edge of the backyard pool. This triumph of efficiency pleases her the way getting a bargain pleases some people, and she likes to tell about it.

Mrs. Zellen looks especially pleased this morning. "I thought, since the postmen deliver all these cards, that I ought to do something for them too, so I'm sending one to the Postmaster General."

Penny tries not to let her face reveal her thoughts. How can Clifford stand this, she wonders. Mrs. Zellen latched on to the religion Clifford brought home from college and made a mockery of it, but all he has ever said to Penny is that it's a good thing he became a Christian instead of a Moonie. She guesses that he can't both criticize and honor his mother.

"Be good boys," Penny tells the children. She escapes quickly to her car and drives toward town, passing the church where she goes with Clifford every Sunday and the other church, farther along, that's the polling place where she votes.

Her first stop in town is the Dreamboat, a vast, open sales floor with aisle after aisle of music CDs and tapes. Above the racks of music are posters: travel posters, advertisements, Garfield, the Desirata. She notices one she hasn't seen before: a plainly lettered copy of the first ten amendments to the *U. S. Constitution*, the *Bill of Rights*, which she studied last year in *Morning College*.

At that time she felt unconnected to those rights, like a TV in an unwired house. What good were her rights as a citizen to freedom of speech and religion if she didn't have those rights in her own home? Today she is drawn for a moment to the plain, beautiful language on the unadorned poster. I'm a citizen, too, she thinks.

Instead of browsing, she goes straight to the folk music section where she chooses a tape. She takes it to the attendant and asks him to play a little of it. He hands her the earphones and she sits down.

It is a tape of Greek folk dances, and she is drawn again, just as she was by the TV, into the world that the sound of bouzouki music creates. She closes her eyes and after a moment or two her family fades away and she again sees this morning's dry, mountainous scene with its glimpses of the sparkling sea below. With a little effort she is able to call up Heraclitus himself.

As they walk, she asks him, "Did you have children, Heraclitus?"

"No woman would have married me, the way I lived, and I wouldn't change my habits in order to be married."

"I don't blame you. I wouldn't either. When I got married, I didn't really have any habits to change." As she says this, she realizes that it is not true. There was white bread and bologna and Miracle Whip. It hadn't seemed right at the time to care about food when Clifford cared about God. But Heraclitus is fading from view.

"I liked what you said on TV this morning," she says quickly. "My husband thinks God cares about everything we do."

Heraclitus shakes his head scornfully. "So the fools are still around!"

"He's not really a fool. But I don't agree with him. I don't believe in hell either. I mean, if God doesn't care what we do, why would he punish us? I believe that after we die, maybe we finally go where we belong."

"I always insisted on being where I belonged even when I was alive."

"That must have been a comfort." Then, suddenly, she felt a surge of hysterical laughter, and she added, "The comfort of the Insurrection."

Heraclitus is quiet.

"I'm sorry," she says. "I shouldn't joke with a philosopher. But why don't you tell me, Heraclitus? You're the one who has already died. Am I right about what happens? Is that what they mean by the comfort of the Resurrection?"

At this, Heraclitus fades from view, and no matter how hard she tries to bring him back, he stays away. She opens her eyes to the scene at the Dreamboat. The attendant is studying a textbook on something that looks like esoteric computer stuff. He looks up. "Did you say something?"

"I'd like to buy this tape." She looks again at the *Bill of Rights* but doesn't know where she would hang it.

Outside, Penny realizes she is hungry. It is past one o'clock, and she's been hoping all week to have time to drive to a place on the shore that she likes, so she picks up a cheeseburger, fries and a strawberry shake at the drive-in and heads toward the bay.

She feels herself smiling. She is happy for her mother. Just imagine, Mother as somebody's date! It's hard for her to see how her mother would act on a date, but she hopes it works out. All those years, and her mother working so hard and never having any fun — she hadn't understood when she was little that her mother must have wanted someone in her life besides a daughter, something in her life besides work. She pictures her mother in the juniper berry suit with a man who can joke about an artificial hand and an artificial breast.

The shore is not far away. Penny parks the car, leaving her shoes in the front seat. She follows some broken steps that lead up a hill to a tumbled chimney at one end of a charred foundation. Someone lived here once, warmed himself at the fire, planted beach plums and Russian olive shrubs that still stand. Penny has no idea how long ago. She walks around the remains of the house, then back down the steps. At the waterline, mussels cluster and hang on the submerged timbers of a ruined jetty. Some distance around the curve of the bay is the mouth of a creek. Sometimes she sees a swimmer there, but not today. Closer in, an egret is fishing.

Penny sits in a hollow on the sand to eat her lunch. The sky has changed now from clear to blue to cloudy, and with the sun gone, the hot June temperature has dropped a few degrees. This change feels restful and Penny leans back on the sand.

The sounds of the water lull her to sleep. After a few moments she awakens with a start when she feels herself being sprinkled with light raindrops. She opens her eyes and faces the swelling breeze that carries the rain before it. She looks down the bay through the rain advancing like a billow of smoke between the grays of sky and sea. From the creek's mouth something catches her eye. The swimmer. For a moment she watches as both the swimmer and the rain advance. No one but us, she thinks. *Morning College. Contemporary American Poets.* Wallace's "Swimmer in the Rain" who thinks he is alone. The pleasure of claiming the poem by connecting with it makes her smile. But she does not want to break into the swimmer's solitude, so she turns away from the shore.

On the way home she slips her new cassette into the stereo and rolls open the windows to enjoy the rain. Mist blows into the car where it heightens the sound of the bouzouki. Penny closes her eyes for a moment at a stoplight, and Heraclitus appears. He pops an olive into his mouth; her own mouth tastes it. She drives to the post office, where she mails all of her mother-in-law's cards except the one to the Postmaster General, which she hides at the bottom of her purse.

When she passes the church where she goes to vote, she hears herself say aloud, "I'm going to this church next Sunday." Surprised, she speaks the line again, rehearsing.

But it is not until after the children are asleep, when she and Clifford are getting ready for bed, that she actually makes her speech. Her voice sounds small as she begins. "Clifford," she says. She speaks up, trying to sound self-assured. "Clifford, I'm going to the other church next Sunday."

His eyes look bewildered above the smile. "This sounds like something we should take to the Lord." He drops his pillow to the floor beside the bed and offers Penny hers.

She kneels for a moment, but then stands up. Clifford stops praying and looks up at her.

"Their service starts at 9:30 too," she says. As she speaks, she feels the most amazing sensation, as though she were getting both larger and lighter. "Either you can drop me off or I'll take the other car, whichever you'd rather."

Clifford starts to rise, but as he does so a cramp in his foot seizes him. His big toe stands out and up, and he hops barefoot around the bed, his look of smiling bewilderment replaced for a moment by a look of pain. When he loses his balance and stumbles, she thinks of asking if he'd like his toe sucked, but her freedom of speech fails her. Give it time, she tells herself.

∧∧∨∧∨∧

The Knitting Nancy

I was on my way to the grocery store this morning when the idea came to mind how to make the day special. "Use what you have, Bell," my papa would have said, and memories are what I have.

The repository of the family memories: that's what they always called me. "Bell, which Christmas was it…?" I always knew the answer, too, and with more details than anyone wanted to hear. Oh, I was smart. Not that as I grew up I wouldn't have traded gray matter for blonde hair and one of those figures that they make the clothes for. But the figure would have been long gone by now. The brains are still with me.

I'm sure I made a fine sight, creeping along to the store this morning, so hunched over that the doctor has to take my height with a tape measure. I always wear boots, and I watch my step for fear of a fall. The pavement is heaved up with tree roots, and even with the wind hinting at spring, there's still some ice. A fall might break my hip, and a broken hip is what I take the greatest pains to avoid, as that could mean a permanent, drastic change of address.

That's why I don't take Ralph with me. Even a little mutt like Ralph pulling on his leash could drag me down. He never gets walked anymore. He has to do his business in the yard, which is mined with it, and I figure that helps keep burglars away.

At the grocery store I bought two bananas and a little jar of peanut butter to add some taste to what Mary Ellen will bring me from Meals on Wheels. I'm supposed to eat what she brings – that's why the doctor signed me up for Meals on Wheels – but I don't always like it.

I'm the last person on Mary Ellen's route. Sometimes she comes in and visits with me for a while. Now and then she slips me a little something extra from her home, too, a slice of corned beef or a twice-baked potato like you wouldn't get from Meals on Wheels, but today I have a treat for her, too. They had cherry tarts on special for Washington's Birthday. I picked out the two nicest for when Mary Ellen comes, and I took a packet of birthday invitations. Oh, and at the check-out counter I waited for the right moment and rattled off *that sentence* before the checker could spoil my day saying it to me. She stood stock still with the words in her mouth like a wad of gum, then she swallowed and said, "Same to yourself." Score one for me, though I don't know which is worse on the ear, *that sentence* or "Same to yourself."

Birthday invitations. The big eight-oh. It has to be special, and I'm perfectly prepared to make do and use what I have, memories, although having to make do has always been my noirest bête noire.

At home, after I got Ralph calmed down – he zips around and round the coffee table until I give him a Dog Yummy – I sat down here at my desk with the invitations and my address books, all five of them, which I keep fastened in order with a rubber band. There are only six invitations. I want to put a limit on this, to keep myself from going over the hill.

Five alphabets full of names. And I remember a face for every one of those names. The oldest address book has tooth marks on the cover, and I remember whose teeth put them there: Papa's dog Luther, the one that, as soon as Papa heard him growl, he'd say, "Bell, stop teasing that dog," without even looking around.

That first book has the family in it. It's my brother Albert I want to invite. Albert owes me a birthday party, and I don't forget it, from the time he was six and I was ten. Mother was upstairs giving birth to Lillian, who came early, while Albert's party was going on downstairs, and I had to be the hostess. My sister Sarah was working for the neighbor lady, and I was next in line. I had to supervise the games instead of playing them, and I had to hand out the prizes: the whistle, the jump rope, the jacks. If Lillian could have waited one more day to get born, I might have won those silver jacks, the way I'd hoped.

Really, Lillian owes me the party, not Albert, but Lillian didn't live long enough to know about parties.

Albert's addresses are in all five books, including his last one here in Columbus. But I recall what the Albert who lived here was like. An old grouch that you felt too sorry for to get mad at because of the cancer in his bone marrow. Still ranting about how Roosevelt was responsible for the hippies and the bums on welfare letting the rest of us pay their way. I don't like that Albert, so I'll use the address in Centerville where he lived when he was first married and still had hopes. He was at his best then. Hopes make all the difference, don't they?

Ralph hears me sighing and starts around the coffee table. He's a good dog; he never lets me sit long enough to stiffen up. I ignore him until he's burned off the last Yummy before I get up and give him another one. We keep each other in good shape.

While I'm up I set out the plates for Mary Ellen's and my cherry tarts. I don't want to get so deep in memories that I forget to take care of the real event.

The next person to come to mind is Susannah, my neighbor from forty years ago, from where the cherry tree grew right into the fence, and the two of us canned cherries together every June until Susannah moved west. The best years of my life ended when that moving van pulled away. Every time I walked out that back door and saw the blue jays gobbling up those cherries, it hit me all over again that Susannah was gone. The people who moved in were good neighbors, but the woman wasn't Susannah, who could get things done, who could say, "Let's make dresses today," and we'd go shop for the goods and then spend the day cutting and pinning and sewing up the darts and tacking on the lace. Susannah wasn't the kind of person who had to make do, and neither was I when she was around.

Who else? I remember everyone I ever knew. My girlfriends who had families – and the one who stayed single and became a businesswoman instead, wearing gray gabardine suits to businesswomen's luncheons at the Tea Room. When the models came to her table, she had the right to ask the price, since she could have paid it if she'd wanted. I was with her the day she bought a gray squirrel jacket without any more thought than I'd have given to buying an extra pair of stockings.

Clear as a Bell, that's me. That's the reason I took the final "e" off my name, that and my looks – a belle I'm not. I used to wonder what good being the repository of memories did me. I got A's in school – I still get A's when I take the mail order courses – but being smart never helped me accomplish much of anything or got me a squirrel jacket.

But rich memories are what I have, and I've come to appreciate their value. They're like music; they occupy the mind without causing trouble. They're better than accomplishments, which use up resources and claw each other for top honors with the rest of us in the way. A tune you can hum doesn't make acid rain or war, and neither does a memory, like the memory of my first husband, for instance.

His name was Ralph, and we got divorced in 1934, but it's from 1925 that I want to call him up. We were living in a rooming house then, in a big second-floor room all fresh in orchid and green, and we had high hopes. We'd lie in the bed under those big orchid roses and make plans. I remember our visions of the future as well as I do what actually happened. We were going to buy a farm and a two-story house with lightning rods and raise Leghorns and Rhode Island Reds and have a garden where we grew only the vegetables we liked. But as things worked out, we didn't plant a hill of beans; we didn't even have a house to fight over when he left, let alone any chickens.

Ralph blamed everything on the Depression. "We should have wished for what was possible," he said. "That's what people have to make do with anyway." That was his philosophy. A Depression-type philosophy if I ever heard one – depressing. Always making do. What does a wish matter, if you can only wish for the possible? If you're going to wish at all, why not wish for what you really want?

I was a wisher, all right, when I was a girl. Straggle-haired and barefoot, always wanting. Wanting lace on my dresses – wasn't that silly? – and my mother didn't have time, not with all those babies. I've never been able to look at a pregnant body without turning my head away and feeling crowded, if you know what I mean, like in movies where the Thing swells to fill all the space, and then I have the awful wish for the birth to be so terrible that the woman will make sure it's the last one.

"Lace is extra, and if you want it, you'll have to crochet it and sew it on yourself," my mother said. And I planned to do it. But something always happened. Either I didn't get it crocheted or I didn't get it sewed on. And Mother was too busy to help.

Just thinking about Mother puts me back home with her in my favorite soap bubble of a memory, helping her hang out the wash, handing her each diaper, each sock, each undershirt, each towel and wash rag, handing her the clothespins, fetching the clothes prop. "Be careful," Mother would call. "Watch for splinters." That clothes prop had splinters thick as toothpicks.

But it wasn't the clothes prop that got me, it was the pears. One end of the line was tied to the pear tree, and in late summer the ground was littered with fallen pears crawling with bees. One day I stepped on a pear and got a bee sting on my toe. Mother carried me inside, big as I was, pulled the stinger away, and put baking soda where it hurt. Then she took an empty spool, pounded four thin nails into it with the heel of her shoe and made me a knitting nancy. She taught me how to weave the thread around the nails so that the knitted cord went through the hole in the spool. No one interrupted. No one cried or needed Mother. When we were finished, we'd used so much time that the rest of the wash had started to dry in the basket and Mother had to wet it before we went back outdoors to finish hanging it up.

After that I planned to decorate all my clothes with cord from the knitting nancy. I would make golden thread like the princesses of old and have beautiful dresses instead of Sarah's hand-me-downs.

The cord in the knitting nancy grew longer than the clothes prop, and I gathered it up and kept in my drawer. Mother was always going to show me how to cut it off, but not right then, and every time I remember it, I get all loose at the seams and helpless, as though I ought to get it out, filthy and old as it is, and finish all those dresses that are nothing but memories now.

Not that there's anything wrong with memories, but when they're all you have, you've nothing to leave behind. On the days when I feel hopeful, I think that maybe you can take them with you. I think that death is like the life I'm living now, only more so. You're alone with your memories, whatever they are. Nothing new would happen, of course, there would be no contact between people, you'd be all alone forever, but I could stand that: I wouldn't have to listen to people brag about their accomplishments. Each person's supply of memories is puffy and round, like a little round cloud, most of them small because people forget. Someday, when all the clouds are in place, gravity will start tugging at their centers, and a wind will come up and the center of each one will be pulled into a funnel cloud and they'll all touch down at the same time, and there will be God complete with what He's given each of us.

Ralph must sense it when I think about the afterlife. He gets all anxious and starts in again and brings me down to earth. I have to tell him that we're not ready for the afterlife just yet and pay some attention to him and give him a Yummy.

Three invitations done: my brother and my neighbor and my first husband Ralph. The next is for my second husband, whose name was Ralph, too. It was during the war that I finished raising the four sons he brought with him. I'd learned my lesson by then and didn't hope for too much from that marriage, but it turned out well. Taking care of children was something I knew how to do, and my neighbor Susannah was there.

After that second husband Ralph died, I always said I couldn't get married again unless I found a third Ralph, and since I never found one, I never married again. But I did start naming my dogs Ralph about that time. I'd gotten used to a Ralph around the house.

Who else would I want at my party? The address books were supposed to prompt me, but the person I really want isn't listed. It's Mother, my mother, and she died when I was only twelve. What would that be like? A reunion, with me eighty years old and Mother forty years younger?

Remembering my mother always makes my body feel different. I try to sit up straight so Mother won't have to remind me. "You were right," I'd have to say. "I got a hump like Grandma."

I should have listened to her. But it wouldn't have done any good, would it? People didn't know, then, that you also have to drink milk and eat ground oyster shells and never stop having periods.

All of a sudden I'm crying. Ralphie whines. I get up and walk around. "Here I go," I say to Ralph. "I start to do something fun, and all I get is a crying jag." Good old Ralph follows me. He knows, he knows.

"What I really want is to see my mother again," I tell him. I'd even be willing to hear her say 'I told you so' about sitting up straight. She would have understood, if she'd lived longer. She'd have realized that you can't keep it on your mind to sit up straight every minute for eighty years. It's trying to defy gravity. I read once that if you don't fall young, you sink as you get old. I'd like to tell that to Mother. Gravity's going to get you, one way or another.

I want to talk to Mother about that wish I had, too, about that birth being the last one. I certainly didn't mean for it to be so bad she'd die. She must have wanted it to be the last one, too. She might have even wanted mine to be the last one. I worried for years that my wishing made it happen, but I've come to realize that even if wishes generally could have an effect like that, mine couldn't. Nothing ever comes of my wishes. The best I can do is what my husband Ralph always recommended, to make do with what I have.

Ralphie and I are at the window now and we look out together, Ralphie with his front paws on the windowsill. He's no doubt thinking about adding another pile of dog-do to the minefield, but I'm looking at the oak tree with its brown leaves shaking in the wind.

Can it be that I will hang on past a hundred and go to my grave still crying for my mother? That I'll be there in my little cloud of memory with its wish at the center, funneling to God and saying, "That's how it's been for me."

Well. We stand at the window for a while, Ralphie and I, then I wipe my eyes. It's almost time for Mary Ellen and Meals on Wheels. It's a treat for me when Mary Ellen comes. She's good to me, takes time to visit, and brings me a little something extra. I go through the living room and straighten the picture that shakes crooked when the planes fly over. I fold up the morning paper and lay it on the stack. I wipe my face with a wet paper towel and put a dab of powder on my nose.

I watch at the window and see her get out of the car. She has only the one box, the one from Meals on Wheels, so there won't be anything extra today, but that's all right. I have the cherry tarts set out for us. When the doorbell rings and Ralph runs barking, I'm ready, with my chin as high as it goes. A gust of wind catches the door and it opens so wide I have to hold Ralph back with my foot.

Then I see that the beige-coated woman holding the Meals on Wheels box is not Mary Ellen. I stand there gaping at her, surprised.

"Mary Ellen's off this week." The woman hands me the box and steps back toward the stairs. "I'm taking her route. But she'll be back next Monday." She's in a hurry, that one, you can tell. No extra visiting for her. "You have a nice day now," she says.

I push the door closed and lean on it. "Damn," I tell Ralph. "Damn, damn, damn." I have to stand here a minute and catch my breath. "Same to yourself," I mutter.

Then I carry the box to the kitchen and eat, just like I always do, with a little peanut butter on the bread to add some taste. When I put one of the cherry tarts down for Ralphie, he looks up at me to make sure I really mean it. "Cheers," I say to him. "We can always make do, can't we? That's what it's all about, isn't it?"

/\.\/\.\/\.\

Gorgonzola Suns

One of the days that Hank enjoyed most was the Sunday of the River-bank Art Fair. Much of his pleasure stemmed from its really being Carla's day. He worked at the fair for her sake. She was the artist, not he. Her paintings, not his, were displayed at the booth, her booth. He could have fun and be supportive at the same time.

Carla, however, saw it differently. When Hank rattled the closet door fumbling for his pants at first light, she opened her eyes, then closed them again. It was really Hank's day, she thought. He was the one who got a boot out of it, shopping around, ordering things to stock the store, his store. If she had to go through the misery of watching people pass the booth without buying, then he could do the work of loading while she rested up for the ordeal.

Knowing she was tired, he let her sleep until the last possible moment. She'd been putting in long hours with him at the store, long hours painting, more long hours keeping house, though he helped, he helped; he was no slob. At least she was tired from interesting work, he thought. His first wife's tiredness had been from boredom, being alone with little children all day while he pursued promotions.

So Carla half-snoozed while Hank carried everything out: racks, paintings, prints; cooler and beer; lunch. Back and forth, house to car. Display racks; folding chairs. She could hear him under the window stepping out of his way each trip to skirt the stump he had hit yesterday with the lawnmower. There was a yellowjackets' nest in the stump. Though she felt guilty about not helping, she was glued to the bed postponing anxiety. Only later, setting up at the fair, would she be able to muster any warmth for the project, when the excitement

37

of the crowd would let her hope that maybe, just maybe, she would make a real sale this time.

∧∧∧∧∧

They worked together setting up their site at the top of the river bank. "What do you think?" Hank placed the shadowed nude on a display rack. "Should we hang it here in front to entice people?" The shadowed nude was his favorite. He had asked her to overprice it to make sure it wouldn't sell.

Carla's fingers twisted picture wire onto her own favorite, her most recent painting. "How about his one?"

"It's lovely," he said, "but the nude's an eye-catcher. You have to prostitute yourself a little when you're selling." Then, in a sudden flash of theatrics, he dropped to his knees and said, "May I be your pimp, young lady?"

He was so appealing there on his knees, all grizzled beard and grizzled forearms, all strong shoulders and broad chest, that she ignored the disquiet his words provoked and smiled at the sight of him instead.

He stood up slowly and grunted. "The knees give out before the heart does," he said. "This generation gap's killing me."

She didn't like that kind of talk. "I'll finish setting up. Go look at the fair."

"I want a beer. You go find out who's here and what I should look for."

∧∧∧∧∧

Carla moved upstream. All along the riverbank people were examining pots and paintings, metalwork and macramé, with the river like the background of a Seurat.

She concentrated on the scene as a whole, trying to think in painterly terms, seeing instead of feeling, but she couldn't maintain it. She could see too well.

She could see all the people crowded around Joann's booth. In Carla's mind she saw them carry off paintings like ants with a crumbled cookie, stripping the booth bare of those beautifully-executed but trite little floral watercolors that Joann turned out by the dozen to meet the demand.

She hurried past the booth, waving only at the last minute to Joann.

But the worst was over. Now she could look around and find things for Hank.

/\/\/\/\/\

A man and woman with a toddler approached the booth. Hank nodded to the man, whose shirted belly draped his fly like an apron full of rising dough. He too had a young wife, but in this marriage there was a child. Carla would change her mind and want a child one day, Hank was sure of it. And what would he do then?

"Murky, aren't they," said the man to his wife. "Every color looks like black."

She was pushing the empty stroller and examining the paintings, while the child, a boy, hung on his father's forefinger for balance.

"Here's one that's brighter," she said. It was the brick facade of a house, its windowsills filled with geraniums in clay pots. The murkiness was contained behind the window. "How do you like this one?"

"How much?" the man asked Hank.

"The prices are on the frames."

He looked at the sticker. "Ummm. Fine painting." They walked on, the little boy's bare toes gripping the grass for traction.

Hank switched the geraniums to a less prominent spot and silently damned the couple to a philistine hell.

With all these paintings before him at once he noticed something he had missed before, that in each of Carla's large works there was a space somewhere, like a door left open for escape. It was most noticeable in the one that had started as a nude with herself as model and was painted over several times, the background more and more lush, until the space where she as subject had been was now mysteriously empty. It was as though she had painted herself into a corner, risen off the floor, then disappeared. Amazing, he thought.

His thoughts then shunted to the concern he carried with him always: that she wouldn't stay. She needs me now, he thought. I can still help her. But it won't be long until she starts getting the recognition she deserves. And when that happens and she can paint with some assurance that her work will have a place to hang besides the store, she'll have time to think about a child. She's going to notice that I'm in my fifties with three grown kids and a vasectomy. She's going to notice that she's painted herself into a corner.

Hank, with effort, then brought himself back to the here-and-now of the fair. He opened a beer and walked next door to a pottery booth where, along with the usual ashtrays and honey jars, there was a large sculpture that he wanted to examine.

"How the hell does this work?" The piece consisted of two high ceramic walls set at right angles and latticed in pigeonholes like the grid of a crossword puzzle. A few of the pigeonholes were filled in solid. A few more held animal figures. Most were empty. The sculpture didn't look as though it could stand up, let alone have been fired.

One of the two young men at the booth lifted an otter from an open pigeonhole. "It comes apart, see? It's got rods inside for support." He nodded toward the other man. "He's been working on that sucker forever, and the more he adds, the worse it gets to drag around."

"And the more unsaleable," Hank observed.

"It's not for sale," said the smaller man. Hank noticed that his right eye looked left, while the left one looked straight ahead. "I just work on it for fun. I bring it along to the fairs to add interest to the booth. People get tired of pots. That may be all they want to buy, but they want something different to look at."

"True," said Hank. The Brown House, his store, was filled with just such a mix of the useful and the interesting.

He opened his wallet and handed the young man a Brown House card. "Call me when it's finished," he said. "I'd like to display it."

"Thanks anyway." The young man pocketed the card. "I appreciate the honor. But it's going to be a long time before it's finished. Maybe never."

"That's okay," said Hank. "Take all the time you need. Just keep me in mind."

Back in his chair with another beer he was willing to bet that the prospect of gallery space would stimulate work on the sculpture. "Six months," he thought. "Maybe less."

He saw yellow shorts and a yellow shirt coming his way. Long brown legs. Black hair in a thick braid, tendrils loose around the face he loved. She still looked tired.

"Anything happen?" she asked.

"A couple priced the geraniums."

"Well why'd you hide them, then?" She put the painting back where it had been.

"I didn't like their attitude."

She shrugged. "Anything else?"

"I spent some time over there." He nodded toward the next booth. "If we're lucky, we'll get that sculpture for the store."

She sat down and picked up her magazine, the latest *Vogue*. "Who all's here?"

"Wally and Bea and John," she said. "Joann's right over there."

Hank put his hands to the sides of his face like blinders.

"Where the crowd is."

"I don't want to know about Joann."

"She's a fact of life." Carla looked critically at her own display.

"Hey, I noticed something interesting while you were gone," said Hank. "Look at this." He showed her the disappearance point in one of the paintings. "It looks like a hole," he said. "Almost all of them have it somewhere. An escape hatch." He waited, hoping she would read his mind and guess that he'd like some reassurance.

"It's just the same old problem I have with perspective," she said. "It's a bore-ass." She changed the subject. "There's a macramé booth over by the big tree. Big pieces, woven in the round, like sculpture."

"I'll take a look. Did you find anything we have to have?"

She held up three fingers and settled down with the magazine.

ᴧᴧᴧᴧᴧ

She had seen the whole fair, and most of it was awful. Out-of-the-tube still lifes, purple mountain majesties, crocheted dolls to put over the extra roll of toilet paper. She saw a man buying a picture of a covered bridge and she knew just where it would hang: over the fake leather love seat.

Of course there were some good things too. The macramé. She talked with people she knew from art school. She took care of some business she had with her friend John, the metal sculptor. There were the local artists, loyal to the fair, who continued to bring their work year after year.

They don't belong here, she thought, and neither do I. I'm not living the right life if I'm envious of people like Joann.

Carla opened her magazine to blot out the here-and-now.

/\/\/\/\/\/\

Hank moved with the flow of people. The sun was getting hot, high in the sky. Adolescent boys jostled each other, their skin-tight jeans shrunk tighter by river water. Smaller children danced closer and closer to the edge. Hank breathed deeply, letting the odors of sweat, mowed grass, and spilled beer entertain his nostrils.

Ahead he saw Bea's booth. Scrupulously-done nature scenes: a few maple leaves, a chicory plant, a cedar waxwing, gray fungi on grayer bark. He nodded to Bea and looked around until he saw the picture he wanted.

It was large, browns and whites, a crane relaxed as no human could relax, one foot drawn up from the pebbly waterline. He looked at the price tag: NFS. "But that's the one I have to have," he complained. "The store has an empty spot for that painting."

"Tough titty," Bea answered. "That one's going to win 'Best of show' at the Carleton and the price will immediately skyrocket and a fabulously rich ninety year old man in very poor health is going to buy it," she came up for breath, "and *me* — and then die the next week and I can quit this stuff and have orgies in Rio."

"Send me a card from Rio."

"Say, I saw Carla's booth. Nice. Very nice. When did she paint the two portraits?"

"They're new. She just finished the big one in time for the fair."

"I'd say she's doing beautifully," said Bea. "With the store and all. How's she coming with her beauty shop ambition?"

"With what?"

"She used to say she'd like to do the beauty shop thing."

"You mean paint beauty shops? Use a beauty shop as a gallery?"

Bea laughed at him. "I mean get her hair done every week. I know, it doesn't sound like Carla. I mean, after all, the way she wears her hair. It's perfect as it is."

Hank shook his head. "Carla wouldn't be caught dead in a beauty shop."

"Don't be too sure."

Then Bea's attention went to a couple who were considering the waxwing. She waved an absent-minded goodbye to Hank, who was picturing Carla, ludicrous in purple curlers.

Farther along, a booth of batiks. A new exhibitor. Interesting. Hank was drawn to a rust and yellow that suggested two figures cut from a string of fold-and-cut dollies, each one blessed by the rays of its own Gorgonzola sun. Probably one of Carla's choices. Maybe they could swap a painting for it. He'd like to own it, not just keep it at the store to sell to someone else, but money was scarce.

He walked on, looking, greeting friends. He loved these fairs: the pottery, each strawberry colander, each pie plate shaped and glazed by a hand that gave thought; the paintings, each one starting as a problem that nagged, as a piece of cloth stretched on pieces of wood, as a plane surface to be filled with intimations of all four dimensions. If he were to fall into an excess of sentiment, he knew it would happen here.

He was beginning to feel tired now, but a few booths down he saw John Carroll with his brass and copper pieces. He had to look at the whole display and admire those Rube Goldberg sculptures with absurd reaction chains like the Mouse Trap game. In addition to the playthings, John made intricate sheet metal fountains along the same line. Hank had wanted one of those fountains for a long time, still did, that twisted one right there, with wheels and basins and flapping triangles made of copper that would discolor gorgeously with time. "I'm drooling," he said.

"Sorry," answered John. "Today was the day. I sold it."

"Traitor!"

"It's getting a good home."

Hank hurried now to get back. At his own booth he noticed a "sold" sign on the shadowed nude. Oh she would be happy! But the nude? His favorite?

Just in time to spare him from strained congratulations Wally Barnes came up and peered at the nude. "I like this," he said. "It's new, isn't it?" Wally had been a part time instructor at the art school when Carla was a student.

"No it's not," said Carla. "It's not sold either. I just put a 'sold' sign on it to make people think I was worth collecting."

"That's a relief," said Hank.

Carla gave him a look.

She's going to have to develop a thicker skin, he thought.

Wally sat down on the grass. Hank opened the cooler and offered sandwiches around, unwrapping one for himself.

"Maybe that's what keeps a person moving ahead," said Wally, chewing bread and ham. "Not selling. I'm in a rut. I worked up a clientele and now I'm stuck with it."

"How about buying that painting you liked?" said Hank.

"Huh-uh. I don't buy paintings. See you at the shows." He struggled to his feet and left, stuffing the sandwich crust into his mouth.

Hank and Carla looked at each other. She reached for her magazine.

"I found one of the things you want," he said, hoping to cheer her up.

She waited, beyond cheering.

"The batik – the two figures under the two suns. There's another one that I lust after, Bea's crane, but she says it's going to feed her own lust." Bea's crane, and the fountain, of course, but he has wanted the fountain for years.

"Did you see the rope things?"

"They're big, aren't they? She was busy so I didn't talk to her about one for the store. Go on out and look around some more. Get what you want, but get it cheap."

"Get-it-cheap is my middle name." She put her magazine under the chair and left.

ʌʌʌʌʌ

Earlier, while Carla was sitting at the booth immersed in *Vogue*, she'd had a visitor.

"Suzy, I swear," a voice had said. "Aren't you Suzy Nichols?"

Carla had looked up into a face from ten years ago. It took her a while to answer. She wasn't Suzy Nichols any longer. "Well for heaven's sake," she said. "Evelyn." Her mind searched through a string of nightclub gigs in a string of cities. "I can't remember where," she said. "I can see you just as plain, but I can't think where it was." She made her voice polite but not friendly. She was Carla Gordon now and did not want to be dragged back into being Suzy Nichols.

"Santa Fe," said Evelyn. "The Cliff Dweller. It closed down a little later. Right before I moved here to take care of my mother." She sat down in the other folding chair. "You haven't changed a bit," she said. "Still the artiste."

Carla swallowed. The artiste. Oh God. "Was I doing art then? What I remember is going from one dark club to the next, and Jeff playing, and then going on to somewhere else."

"You sat with a tablet and some pencils and a big eraser and drew the whole time you were there," said Evelyn. "Every time you came. I still have the one you drew of me. I don't know what you did other places, but at the Cliff Dweller you made a nice little pot drawing the customers."

Carla laughed bitterly. "Real progress," she said.

"It looks like you're doing all right for yourself." Evelyn glanced around at the display, then stood up and examined the new portrait more carefully. "Carla Gordon. Is that your artist name?"

"That's the name I go by now." Carla's attention was partly diverted by a woman studying the front row of paintings. A potential customer.

"Whatever became of Jeff? He still playing?"

"We split up. I don't know where he is."

"Are you married again?"

"Yes I am. Hank and I got married three years ago."

"And who's Hank? Not another musician I hope."

"No. Hank owns the Brown House. It's a store here that specializes in crafts and fine arts." The potential customer had moved closer now and was looking at the paintings in the back row.

"Oh *that* place. You really *have* come up in the world."

The skin on Carla's face felt tight. "I don't know about coming up in the world," she said. "But Hank's a good husband."

"That's up," said Evelyn. "I'm still tending bar. I'd like to find a good husband and get off my feet."

Carla rose. This conversation had to end. She spoke to the customer, "Let me know if you have any questions."

Evelyn stood up too. "Drop in some time. Bring your husband," she said. "I work at the Derby. Seven till two."

Carla willed the customer to buy, but it didn't happen. The customer departed, and after a little more chitchat, so did Evelyn, leaving Carla with a magazine that no longer helped to protect her.

∿∿∿∿

Hank saw the ceramicist next door playing solitaire and drinking from a quart bottle of Budweiser. "I'll watch your booth," he said. "Go take a look around."

"Thanks," was the answer. "Think I'll go for a swim instead." He chug-a-lugged the beer, then took off his boots and added them to those of the other man.

"Be sure to see the fair too," advised Hank. "If you look close, you can find some good things out there."

The young man pulled off his shirt to reveal a torso still skinny, like a child's. "I don't give a damn about art," he said. He looked at Hank with his straight left eye. "I'd rather clean hog pens any day than walk around and gawk at this drivel." He started for the river.

"Whoa," said Hank. "How come this, then?" He pointed to the ceramic walls.

"That's different. That's just for fun."

Hank watched him slide down the riverbank and ease himself into the water. He walked over again to the sculpture. Just for fun. Would it still be fun when the kid got serious? He hoped so.

A little later the other ceramicist returned, wet and happy, and in a moment Carla appeared. She carried a red wooly macramé piece, holding it draped high so it wouldn't drag the ground. "The batik was gone," she said, "but I worked out a deal for this. I give John Carroll the geraniums and the shadowed nude and he gives Alex – that's her name, Alex – one of those perpetual motions of his, and I get the macramé."

"You're giving away the nude?" He couldn't believe what she had done.

"I might as well." Her braid had come loose and her hair was stuck in the sweat on her face and neck. "John's going to pick it up this evening after the fair."

"Carla!" There was no place in the house she could possibly hang that macramé. And it was worth far less than even one of the two paintings she was giving up for it. "Couldn't you have held out for a trade on the geraniums and kept the nude? The macramé is good, but not that good."

"Let's go home," she said. Her voice was listless. She leaned two of the larger paintings against the car.

He took her hand. "I was looking at everything this morning, and it's remarkable how much better you're painting than even a year ago."

"That doesn't help. I'm thirty-four years old. Nobody asks some-one my age, 'Are you painting better than you used to?' They ask, 'What have you sold recently?'"

"Sure," he said, "you're decidedly long in the tooth. But that's the kind of question to ask a salesman. That's what you should be asking *me*, not yourself."

"Couldn't we go? The fair's almost over."

Silently Hank and Carla dismantled the booth, loaded and left, driving slowly past the diminishing crowd.

Once home, Carla picked up the macramé and disappeared into the house. Hank stayed and took his time unloading. He carried the card table and chairs inside and took them to the basement past the closed bathroom door. The shower was running.

As he had carried them all out this morning, he carried them all back this evening. Inside, he picked out the shadowed nude and hung it in its place over the hump-backed trunk, then started upstairs to the studio with a box of prints.

Carla emerged from the bedroom, fresh in clean shorts and shirt, with her hair wet and sleek. She walked to the stack of paintings leaning against the trunk, frowned at the first one, stood it aside and frowned at the next.

Hank waited until she looked at him. "Honey, what's the trouble?" He knew he shouldn't ask her questions like that, but he didn't stop himself in time.

She jerked as though touched with a hot wire, but her voice was impassive. "The trouble is that I'm never going to make it." She placed another painting on top of the third and frowned at it too. "I knew when I painted this that it wasn't any good." It was another nude, a blue one. "The only thing right about it is the color."

"And the color is the only reason it hasn't sold. You're palette's different."

"If I were any good, someone would have noticed by now."

"Carla, this conversation's been beaten to a pulp."

She took the shadowed nude off the wall and stood it against the trunk.

Hank started toward her but stopped as though he had run into an invisible electric fence. "Let's go out and get something to eat and forget about it for a while."

"We're not going anywhere! Not when I can't even afford decent underwear. Somebody around here has to think about money. If I'm too uptight about sales, it might just be because we need the goddamned money."

"For Christ's sake, go buy some underwear."

"Go buy some underwear! And a new roof for the house? If you took more care, maybe I wouldn't have to worry about these things."

"Goddammit, I do take care! Think about it! Do you think you'd be painting at all if I hadn't been taking care? Didn't I see you through art school? What kind of care do you want, anyway?"

Instead of answering, she stared at him in a challenging way.

"What's all this about?" he asked. "I know. You've decided you want to quit work at the store and start a family. Well, you knew when you married me that I couldn't make that happen."

"I wish you'd quit harping on that. I said I didn't like taking care of children, and I meant it. Stop bringing it up every time we have a fight."

"Well, what *are* you fighting about? Does this have anything to do with wanting to go to the beauty shop?"

"You're out of your mind!"

"I heard from a reliable source that your idea of the real thing was to get your hair done every week."

"That's ridiculous. I'd like to be able to afford it, but...'

He interrupted. "It's not like you to be so hung up on money."

Anger flared in her face. "Don't *you* tell *me* what I'm like. You don't understand a thing about what I'm like."

"I sure don't. Not if you're like those women who want to fritter their lives away at the beauty shop."

"When have I ever had a chance to fritter? I work my ass off. I'd love to do a little frittering for a change. What's so terrible about that?"

A knock sounded at the screen door followed by a man's voice: "Should I walk around the block and come back later?"

Carla became hospitable at once. "John! Come in." She hurried to open the screen. "We were just livening up a dull Sunday evening."

"Don't let me interrupt anything." He came inside cautiously, carrying a carton with a piece of cotton blanket over the top. His arm was stuck between the spokes of two copper wheels. "Where do you want this disasterpiece?"

Carla's eyes shifted between John and Hank. "Maybe John would like a drink." She glanced pointedly toward the kitchen.

Hank looked at the box, then at Carla. "How about a beer, John?"

"Thanks," said John. "I saw you leave and figured the heat was getting to you."

When he came back with three beers, John was saying, "The fair closed down. You left while it was happening."

"While what was happening?"

"There was a guy drowned. Went swimming and drowned."

"Oh Lord," said Carla. "Who was it? How'd it happen?"

"The guy in the booth next to you missed his buddy when he'd been gone a while. He went back in the water to find him, and when he didn't show up and didn't show up, he got a lot of people to help, and they found him snagged by the belt on a tree limb."

Hank's vision went black. The kid. The kid with those ceramic walls. Who made them because it was fun. The beer bottle slid gently from his hand and came to rest upright in his lap.

There was a long silence. Then Carla asked for details and John gave them. "I'm sorry to show up here with such a gloomy story."

"Want another beer, anyone?" asked Hank.

"This one's enough, thanks," John answered. He drained the mug and asked Carla, "How'd you do today?"

"I'm quitting," said Carla. Her voice fluttered. "I've had enough of being the artiste. They say that once you start, you can't quit, but that's ridiculous."

Carla's words were audible to Hank, but they sounded distant. He didn't believe what she was saying.

"If you try something and it doesn't make you happy, I say you ought to quit."

Hank spoke from his distant blackness. "Being happy isn't the important thing. People act like being happy is the meaning of life."

"Speak for yourself about the meaning of life," said Carla. "Don't speak for me."

"Who's happy anyway?" said John awkwardly. "If you expect art to make you happy, forget it." He turned his thumb toward the boxes on the floor. "I'm happy you guys took this fountain off my hands and happy for the kick in the butt it gives me to make another one. Maybe a better one. Maybe not, too."

Hank decided he ought to be sociable. "Fountain?" he inquired, though he knew what was in the box. "Did I hear the word 'fountain'?"

"Happy Flag Day," said Carla. "Or whatever." She moved around the coffee table to Hank's chair where she sat on the arm beside him. "Maybe if we dance around it three times, it'll turn into the fountain of youth."

Her words hit him where it hurt.

John stood up. "I'll move along. He took the shadowed nude and looked around for the geraniums. "I'm going to enjoy these."

Hank watched Carla find the geraniums and watched John carry both paintings to the door. Then he stood with Carla at the screen watching John take the paintings to his car.

"Like your present?"

"What can I say? Of course I like it." He noticed the triangular rip in the screen. He had promised to patch it several weeks ago, but the store had been absorbing every spare minute. "Of course I like it." Outside on the lawn the long rays of evening sun caught the waving grass blades where he had left off mowing when the yellowjackets hit him.

"I like it very much," he said, but she was gone. He knelt by the box. The covering of blanket stuck up in points from the cardboard. He removed it and unwrapped the tubing and the triangles, setting them carefully side by side, with the millwheels, on the carpet. He could feel Carla watching him from the doorway, hear the floorboards creak when she went on to the kitchen.

After a while he followed her into the kitchen where she stood at the sink peeling potatoes. He approached and stood behind her, put his arms around her, felt her stiffen.

"What's the matter, honey?" There he went again. Not really a question, a declaration of anxiety.

The half-peeled potato bounced into the sink. The knife followed. She pushed him back hard.

"I hate it," she answered. "I started out doing something for fun and you came along. You came along and took it over. You took it over. You pushed me and pushed me until it wasn't fun anymore. You weren't willing to take the risk of putting yourself on the line so you took over what I was doing." She stopped talking.

He couldn't say anything.

"I never wanted a manager," she said. "A pimp. I wanted a husband. I wanted some fun out of life. Not this constant striving to get *good* enough to sell and then finding out that you also have to be *fashionable*."

He still couldn't say anything.

"And you had to walk out of Foster where you had it made and sink every cent you'd saved into that damned store that takes everything we've got and gives us nothing in return." She dried her hands and headed for the door. "Nothing!"

"Where are you going?" he asked anxiously, following her. In the mirror beside the door he could see his forehead pulled into three furrows that dipped in the middle like a valentine heart.

"For a bike ride," she said from the step.

"I'll come with you. We need to talk."

"Leave me alone," she said. "There's nothing you can say that I want to hear. Nothing you can do that I want done. Leave me alone."

He watched her go down the walk and take her bike out of the shed. When she slammed the shed door, the rusted left half fell off as usual. She ignored it. He closed his eyes for a moment. When he opened them, she was gone. There was no point propping the shed door back up. It would just fall down again.

He walked back to the sink and looked helplessly at the browning potatoes, then into the living room where the paintings stood like orphans.

Around and around the house he walked, then stopped in the bathroom to wash his face. In the mirror he faced the grizzled beard and the wrinkles.

Too much had happened. A day wouldn't hold this much. He felt numb, as though waterlogged, as though weighted down by the drowned man. The sun had fallen below the trees. In the living room he turned on a lamp and picked up Carla's magazine.

I'm going to have to use everything I know, he thought. Take advantage of my age. Remember what it was like. She'll come through, but I can't push. Just listen. He rolled the magazine and hit the back of a chair. "Damn!"

He looked impatiently at his watch. She won't stay out long, he thought. She'll be home by dark. Her bike light doesn't work.

ᴧᴧᴧᴧᴧ

From down the block Carla saw the light on in her living room window. She slowed down, tired from pedaling. Without the motion to cool her she felt sweat stand out on her face and fill her hair.

It shouldn't take a fight, she thought. We shouldn't have to fight to find out these things. I hate being such a bitch, she thought.

She wheeled into the driveway and stopped behind the beech tree where she knew she was still hidden from the house.

There was just enough light for her to see up into the beech, to where the first big branch joined the trunk. A large muscle flexed there under the beech's gray skin. She had drawn it over and over, but she hadn't gotten it right yet. Her eyes went farther out on the limb. That's the problem, she thought. I didn't take it far enough. Once you get into muscle, you have to extend it all the way. You have to take it all the way to where the potential energy stored in the muscle can flow clear to the end, to the end of its reach. She leaned against the trunk to gather herself and rest for a moment before going inside to Hank.

Webs

We were at the supper table one evening the summer I was almost eight when my father, who had come home from the plant bent over and pale around the eyes, cleared his throat and broke the bad news.

"They laid off another bunch of men today," he said. His big hands mumbled over the knife and spoon, the fork. His forehead pinched together, and when Mother gave him a questioning look, he nodded yes.

Mother put down her chicken leg and closed her eyes without saying a word, without even wiping the grease off her fingertips.

My father saw her. His eyes fired up. "If you're praying, don't bother." He sat up straighter and looked like his usual self. "It's not going to help. We're in a depression."

She flashed back, "I wasn't praying, but it might help more than you think. It's possible your attitude's not helping either."

I looked at my spinach and stopped taking breaths. That was what I did to avoid the air that had their fights in it.

"Stop it, Gwennie," said Mother aside to me.

"If there's a God up there, He sure doesn't care about the working man," said my father. "If you want to pray to a God like that, thanks anyway."

Mother closed her eyes again, then opened them. "This didn't happen through any fault of your own." It was not quite a question.

"You're damn right it didn't," he growled. "If the hogs on top hadn't swilled off the cream and gambled it in the stock market, there'd be a cushion against hard times."

She reached her hand out toward him. "You'll find another job,

Clark," she said. "We'll be all right. We can get along on what I make for a while. There's the garden. And you can fish." She swallowed a lump of air. "And if a rainy day really comes, we can use some of the savings."

"Sure, and burn the furniture to keep warm."

Then they stopped talking to each other and concentrated on my noisy celery and my elbows and my foot that kept kicking the table leg.

Later, when my father was reading the paper in the living room and I was helping clean up, Mother said, "I could be more sympathetic if he weren't so grouchy." She poured boiling water from the teakettle over the clean dishes to scald them. "I just wonder if he's that hard to get along with on the job."

I didn't like to take sides, so I kept quiet while I dried the knives and forks and stood the plates on their rims in the cupboard.

It was a Wednesday evening, and Mother decided to go ahead to choir practice in spite of the bad news. "I need to sing," she said. "If I don't sing, I'll cry, and if I cry, I might never stop."

The church was right next door to us. I could hear the choir singing through the open windows. I went outdoors and played by the fence with sopranos made of hollyhocks and tenors made of clothespins. I waved my arms like Mrs. Purcell and sang "Glory Glory" in a high voice and "trampling out the vintage" in a low one. "You can do better," I told the clothespins. "Sing from the diaphragm." That was what Mrs. Purcell said. I didn't know what it meant. I didn't know what being in a depression meant either, or why my parents were always in a fight.

My father said he hadn't bought the house next door to the church for Mother to get herself sucked into hymn-singing and holy-rolling. He had bought it because his mother, my grandma's house was next door to us on the other side. Grandma lived there with my Uncle Waldo, and she took care of me while Mother was at work.

Uncle Waldo had a job spraying roaches. He was fat and red, with broken-out wrists from the poison. He went out every morning in his truck with the statue of a roach on top, and Mother went to her office in her high-heeled shoes and secretary dresses, while my father read the want ads and went looking for work, or stayed home and weeded the vegetable garden, or helped Grandma take care of me.

Mother said thank goodness she had a job, and she'd rather walk the streets than be cooped up with a grouch like him all day.

I felt the same way and could hardly wait to go back to school, except when he forgot about taking care of me and we worked together in the garden. He would push the cultivator down between the rows while I scraped away with a wallpaper scraper to cut the weeds up near the carrots and the onions. He showed me how to dig easy so I wouldn't slice into the potatoes and how to tie up the tomatoes with a strip of rag from an old shirt. He wasn't grouchy then.

We watched the black-and-yellow spider in her big web between the rows of zinnias. She would wait in the center, looking like a flashy medallion on a big lace doily. When an insect touched the web and the spider ran to secure it, my father would say, "Another bug down the hatch!" He told me to go easy when I was weeding. "She needs the web to do her job, Gwennie. Be careful."

It wasn't until we went back in the house that he started taking care of me again and got grouchy.

In the evening Mother would come home and kick off her shoes and change into a housecoat. She would let me help fix supper while we sang "Three Blind Mice" and "Go Tell Aunt Rhody the Old Gray Goose Is Dead" and all the verses of "A Capital Ship for an Ocean Trip Was the Walloping Window Blind." "Singing to keep from crying," she would say.

Uncle Waldo got home next door a little later, and as soon as he washed off the poison and ate the supper Grandma fixed, he would come outside and lift me up on top of his truck. Then he would drive slow up and down the driveway while I pretended I was a cowgirl and the roach was my horse.

There weren't any possibilities for my father in his business, Uncle Waldo said, because everybody had the same idea. Everybody was laid off, and if the boss hired all the people who needed jobs, there wouldn't be enough roaches to go around. But he kept his eyes open and talked to people, and every once in a while he would say to my father, "I heard about something today."

The next day my father would go and wait with a crowd of other men to apply for the job. He would come home mad that he had wasted the money getting there. "That's how the big shots want it," he would say. "A hundred men clawing each other for every one of their lousy damn jobs."

But the church made him even madder. He did his fishing on Sunday morning so he wouldn't have to watch people park their shiny cars in front of our house and go into the church. "They preach do-gooding," he said, "but what drives them is profit. Give the poor a handout, but see to it that they stay poor so they'll work for nothing."

One Sunday he kept me out of Sunday School to go fishing with him. We left the car at the public access and walked through the woods to the lake. "What better heaven could you hope for than right here?" he asked. We found a spot to sit on a tree trunk that had fallen into the water where the crappies liked to hide. "This is what people ought to be concerned about, their own home on earth."

We fished quietly for a while, but then a big motorboat roared by, and he got to talking about the people who owned property around the lake. "The government used taxpayers' money to make this lake and then they let the fat cats take it over," he said. Waves from the motorboat slip-slopped around our log. "It sticks in my craw that she sings for people like that. She's too good for them."

At home he cleaned the crappies and Mother fried them for dinner. By then his fishing mood had worn off and he was himself again, mad at Mother because she had gone to church.

After dinner I told her what he had said. "He thinks you're too good to sing for those people."

She looked surprised and a little pleased, but she shook her head. "He doesn't know them. He's never set foot over there. He thinks they're rich just because he sees them dressed up for church."

He would bawl her out if she even clasped her hands with the fingers woven together. Or if she sat still and looked down at the floor for any length of time. "You don't have to bring their praying home with you!"

Mother said he was imagining things. She said the hand position eased her wrists from all the typing she did, and when she looked at the floor, she was just worrying about the dust balls.

She complained to me. "He ought to help around the house

since he isn't working. It's not right that I should have to do it all."
The dust balls made furry little feet at the table legs and pale gray
roses along the baseboards, and the spider webs made tatting in the
corners.

"I could help," I said.

"I guest you're getting big enough to learn." So she showed me
how to pin a rag around the broom, and I took on the responsibility
for dust and spider webs.

I wondered how the spiders would do their job with me tearing
their webs and dusting them out of the corners.

"Shake the rag outdoors, Gwennie," said my father. "That's where
they belong anyway."

The summer dragged on through July into August. It seemed as
though school would never start. The cantaloupes ripened and the
ironweed bloomed in the weeds by the alley. The leaves fell brown
from the horse chestnut tree, making the wrong color bed for the
spring-pink amaryllis that poked up between them. My father and I
picked corn and beans and filled the tall round basket over and over
with tomatoes.

Mother had to do the canning after supper at night. Water
boiled in the big kettle. The kitchen was hot with steam. We dipped
tomatoes and slipped off the skins, dipped some more and slipped off
the skins. The next night we canned corn, and the floor was slippery
from the kernels that flew all around when Mother pushed the big
knife down the ears. The canner hissed. Mother sang, but even
though I liked to sing with her, I knew it was to keep from crying
about the depression we were in.

"We'll be glad for the food next winter," she said. "Look at it
that way."

Sweat ran down our faces and juice ran up our arms, and cicadas
sang outside in the summer dark. They're in a depression too, I thought.

During the day my father was still home. He did man's work in
the yard and he made dents in the couch cushions. He took more
care of me than I needed.

"Somebody's got to talk some sense into you," he said. "Somebody's got to counteract that rubbish you hear when she takes you

next door." He didn't even call the church a church any longer. He called it "next door."

He criticized Mother for putting money in the collection plate. "They don't need your measly dollar. Churches are rolling in money."

"I pay for what I get," she said. "I need the church. And the money's used for God's work one way or another."

"God's work! If I had God's job, I'd give the working man a leg up instead of taking him for all he's worth."

"You don't have God's job," said Mother. "You don't even have your own job."

He stepped toward her with his eyes squinted up. "I do as good a day's work as any man. I didn't make things the way they are."

She stood her ground and squinted her own eyes. Then they backed away from each other and I took a deep breath.

When he was out of earshot, she said, "Does he think I'm having some kind of summer vacation? Work till I drop, and not a nickel to call my own, and him grouching around the house from morning till night. He never gives my feelings a thought." She moistened her lips and swallowed, then started to sing in a fluttery voice. "Go 'way from my window, go 'way from my door." We sang together. "Go 'way 'way 'way from my bedside and bother me no more, and bother me no more."

In late August the drugstore advertised school supplies. I looked at the long box of crayons that had gold and silver in it. "Wait and see what they provide at school," said Mother. "Then we'll fill in what you need."

The week before school started I was in the bathroom one morning watching my father shave to go out and apply for a job. Uncle Waldo had told him about a plant that had gotten a government contract. "They'll be hiring," he had said. My father stretched his jaw and scraped. I watched him in the mirror. Then I saw his gaze catch something off to the side.

It was the spider in the bathtub. The big black one. It had been there since last night. I saw it before I went to bed. It would climb the side and fall, climb the other side and fall. I had left it alone. I didn't like to kill things, not even scary things, and I didn't have to, since only the webs were my responsibility. It hadn't made a web. It probably couldn't, in the bathtub.

My father looked at the spider for a minute. His forehead pinched together. He tore a piece of toilet paper and held it down in the tub for the spider to climb on. He raised the bathroom window. The sun shone warm on the brick of the church. Then he released the spider and yelled for all the world to hear, "See how it's done, God?" He slammed the bathroom window. "See how it's done?" he yelled again.

I slid off the hamper where I'd been sitting. "Amen," I whispered. I slipped past him into the hall. "Amen."

.\.\.\.\.\

The Frontier

Mr. Liveright's right shoulder had a habit of twitching outside his control, agitating at irregular intervals like a Mexican jumping bean. When he was at home puttering or watching TV, it would be quiet, unless the post office happened to flash across his mind, when it would give a little hop to remind him of his station in life. But it did its serious jerking when he was trying to rise above this station, or else at times like now when it had a long day's work carrying a mail bag to look forward to.

Monday was his heaviest day and today even heavier than most with first of the month bills to deliver. The route was up on the hill and longer than anyone else's – a reward for seniority, he supposed. With his shoulder twitching a counterpoint to the country-western blaring from someone's radio, he stood at his case, sequencing mail and daydreaming about the possibility of a transfer to some illiterate village that shrank each year.

Jim Simpson brought him a load of flats in a canvas cart and walked away without even stopping to torment him. It was always this way on Monday, everyone slack and dull till they woke up. Everyone except Mr. Liveright, who took pride in being cheerful even when his heartburn of resentment simmered.

What did he have to be cheerful about? If the early bird gobbled worms and thrived, then rising before daylight all these years ought to have given him, with his innate potential, a more enviable wing span than he had. He smiled a lot around the post office, a teeth-showing grimace of irritation at the failings of his fellow man, followed by a chuckle to show the fellow man that he was not going to be dangerous this time.

Nights had been late and mornings early recently: from one to five, two to five, sometimes three to five-fifteen, all because of Plum, who could one night promise the good life and the next night threaten the ax, and every night keep him up late. How she could alternate the good life and the ax month after month without fully delivering either, he did not understand. She was an enigma unlike anyone else in his experience.

Plum knew how to live. She had style. Zest. She made it a practice to suck the juice out of life, like rare fruit at the market, pomegranate and kiwi and mango. She knew how to find the best things: the restaurant about to be rated four star, the unknown singer who would soon cut a golden record. She might sniff out a play in a broken-down attic on Ottlesby Avenue where a wino was playing Lear. If anyone else had found such a thing, it would have been a sick joke, but Plum's Lear, this stumbling wretch, would be the real Lear at last. She would dry him out and steer him into a glorious career, world-wide, and when he died, having fulfilled his potential at last, they would put him a crypt next to Shakespeare. That's the kind of woman she was.

And she was willing to share her knowledge of the good life with him, Seaton Liveright, to point out his areas of inadequacy and outline a program for his development. She was making him into the man he was born to be – the man he really wanted to be – and as soon as he had absorbed her lessons, she would marry him and his declining years would be secure in the enjoyment of the good life.

One of her educational projects for him, a lesson in sensuality, had taken place last fall, a picnic during a slow autumn rain in a leafy thicket that was still almost dry. She brought bread in a round loaf, he remembered, sour and black, with soft butter, and some salty fish and a bottle of Liebfraumilch. He had become chilled on the walk to the picnic spot, and the sips of wine on his tongue bit into the chill and stripped away the insulation from his nerves. Everything impinged that day: the impersonal odor of falling leaves and damp earth; Plum's body heat as they lay on his poncho under the umbrella he had hung by its ribs above them; the biting brine of the fish;

the sound of earth sucking rain – and through it all a poignant sense that all of his efforts should strive for an accumulation of such moments, such tones, to make up the chord of his life.

And a thin, stark chord it had been until recently, sounding of octaves and fifths, duty and work, with the richer harmonics straggling in sparse and late. His moments of sensual and aesthetic living had been few before he met Plum. He hadn't known such wealth. Times had been different then; women were different. He had spent thirty years tending his lot in suburbia, forcing himself to take part in the block club and PTA and Scouts, for the sake of family and community, keeping suburbia green and free from crabgrass. None of this had prepared him to be a widower on the town. When his warm little helpmeet Jessica had died, he floundered, not knowing what to do with his time, until Plum came along to show him. She had stimulated him, taught him how to be a man on his own, in and of the world. "You've paid your dues," she said. "You're free now. Enjoy it!" She had led him by the hand to growth groups and fine arts series and to studios and stages where new things were happening.

But Plum exacted her price for lessons in the good life. He had to fetch and carry for her – spade up her garden and patch her roof. Cut wood for her fireplace. And he had better develop his potential or else. It wasn't the work that bothered him, it was the insecurity of "or else." A man paid his dues, and instead of security, all he got was freedom – and freedom was something he hadn't bargained for.

Before Plum, his program for the future had centered only around building a nest egg and fending off personal decline. He invested in blue chip stocks and municipal bonds rated double A; he tithed to the credit union and joined an annuities program. So that he would live long enough to enjoy all this, he installed skid strips and hand rails in the bathtub; he kept his stair treads tacked tight, buckled his seat belt, carried an umbrella. Any program that came along promising to fight the forces of decline he followed: he drank goats' milk, flossed his teeth, worked out, and took the kind of natural vitamins that were pulverized into a grayish-brown meal that smelled like dusty droppings. All he needed now for a secure old age was a woman to share it with him.

He dug into the canvas cart and pulled out a bundle of

brochures from *Save the Eagle*. He noticed with disappointment that *Save the Eagle*, like most "not-for-profit" mailers, used an out-of-date mailing list. But unlike most, this was a worthy endeavor and he wished more of the brochures were deliverable – to wealthy eagle lovers. It was a shame to have to toss these into the "No Obvious Value" bin.

Save the Eagle was one of the causes he was willing to countenance, along with *Save the Redwoods, Save the Rockies* and *Save the Techtonosphere*, which opposed nuclear dumps beneath the earth's crust. He was often urged to expand his portfolio to include mankind, but he refused to put his money in ignoble causes. Mr. Liveright believed the earth would be doing well if it could survive mankind, and he didn't want to help prolong the sojourn of such a threat.

He cased the *Journals* and the *Barronses* and was working on the *Monitors* when temptation became too great. He opened an Eagle folder. The bald eagle was dying out, he read, almost extinct, because profit-craving Mankind had destroyed its nesting spots. Would he, as a friend of the eagle, like to secure forever a spot in Alaska where a family of eagles could nest unhindered by chain saws, bulldozers, and the other encroachments of civilization? His own nesting site in Alaska awaited his check.

He saw Jim Simpson watching him and put the folder down. Jim would make fun of his feeling for the eagle. What did Jim know about aquilology, anyway? He finished casing the mail and went out to deliver it.

Jim was a constant burr in the groin not only because of his vulgarity but also because he was another of Plum's protégés. Whenever Jim took Plum to a wrestling match or a stock car race, he would broadcast it around the post office and Mr. Liveright would suffer humiliation as well as jealousy. The other carriers placed bets: symphony or dog race, egghead or blockhead, Liveright or Simpson? Jim, too, had a key to her house.

When he had finished carrying the route and was getting ready to go home, he picked up an eagle pamphlet and tucked it in his pocket, doing so stealthily so that Jim couldn't see him. He hated to think what obscenities Jim could contrive around the earth's noblest bird. That Plum found anything promising in a man with so little potential bothered him no end. What could she possibly make out of a man who liked dog races? He bared his teeth and chuckled to himself.

That evening Plum stood him up. She had invited him to sit on her L-shaped verandah and eat chicken ragout, but when he arrived, her house was locked. He let himself in. Everything was quiet and gloomy, all polished wood and vacuumed carpet, with a smell of furniture cream, and the chicken still on the carcass. Mr. Liveright waited for a while, drinking an angel-tit he made for himself out of Plum's cognac and some crème de cacao, with a squirt of whipped cream from her refrigerator, remembering that this delightful drink was only one of the many things she had taught him to enjoy. He waited some more and she still didn't come. He couldn't figure out what he could have done – or not done – to deserve this. Baffled, he showed his teeth to whom it may concern and went home to a frozen chicken pot pie.

He should certainly drop Plum. Her favors were exquisite, but indiscriminate; she could play him like a flute – but she played the cello too, and the bongo drums – and even a kazoo like Simpson. But oh, the time spent with her was wonderful; why that day last fall…. No, he couldn't stand to dwell on that. Suppose she had done the same thing with someone else? "Why not?" she would have asked. "Wasn't it fun?"

He was not at all happy with Plum tonight. Always before, when she stood him up, he realized he'd made some unforgivable gaffe and she was withdrawing her favor to teach him a needed lesson. But tonight was different; he had done nothing wrong.

His angry mood brought on memories of her less endearing traits: her habit of talking to strangers and getting involved; her fits of laughter that respected nobody, not even him. Her closet full of dresses that she never tired of adding to. Her disregard of a man's wedding ring: "I'm not responsible for his marriage, am I?" she would say. He felt critical of her and even more critical of himself for putting up with her. It was *not* seemly of her to share with him her enthusiasm for each new man in her life. It was downright rude of her to say he had the soul of a mail bag! His shoulder hopped involuntarily and he cringed at the memories of himself as errand boy, gardener and handyman getting Plum's house primped up for a party where she would laugh and tantalize every man there. Why was he such a door mat to let her walk on him that way? He felt his lip draw up into a teeth-showing. After a moment, he chuckled to remind himself not to be dangerous.

While the pot pie was baking, he took his vitamins and made himself another large angel-tit to kill the taste, a makeshift this time, not as good as the real thing, but not bad either. Sipping it improved his outlook.

He had found Plum; he could find someone else. Single women outnumber single men. Maybe he really could drop her. It wasn't as though he didn't have assets: his nest egg of stocks and savings; a neat brick house with a newly-done kitchen; all his own teeth, and if he was bald, everyone knows that bald men are sexier. His body was an asset too, still quick and muscular, due to years of strenuous work and an absence of bad habits. Both Jessica and Plum, who were vastly different in most respects, admired the ripples under his smooth skin.

He would enjoy displaying these assets, especially the smooth skin, for just the right woman, one who too had been learning about the good life. No dowdy, worn-out soap opera fan for him! He drained his drink and gave his imagination free rein.

How young a woman did he dare consider? Women his own age were all wrapped up in their grandchildren, like Jessica had been. Besides, they were overripe and they sagged – grandmothers. But he didn't want a childless one, fruitless and dry, did he? Forty-five? Maybe. Plum was on her way to forty-five, divorced, two children out of the nest, but she was unique. He couldn't expect to find another like her. Forty sounded more like it. Forty wasn't young any more, but a man's got to be realistic. Many women of forty had interests much like his own, cultural interests, fine arts series and such, but did he want to marry into menopause? Hot flashes and crying jags? He'd been through that once. Thirty-five was probably the right age. A youngish-looking thirty-five year old deserted by a brute of a husband, the poor thing slaving away to support her five children – no, the husband had taken the five children, snatched them from their grieving mother, kidnapped them with the help of a corrupt judge – thank God – leaving her to pine for someone to lavish herself upon. From thirty-five down, his thoughts were vague and archaic: a young woman in trouble with the bank; a girl who wanted to be taught by an experienced man (this fantasy lasted quite a while) – and finally the oven timer rang.

The chicken pot pie burned his tongue and left him hungry. He put another into the oven to bake while he looked at the eagle pamphlet.

It was filled with colorful scenes of cool, green Alaska shoreline, men in glistening ponchos hauling in fish, float planes taking off amidst the boats. Was this the civilization that was encroaching on the eagles? That endless shoreline looked wild enough to him. Overprinted on the brochure, the shadow of a bald eagle peered down, brooding.

In the corner was a blank to fill out with his name and address and a place to check off whether he could afford to be a *Perpetual Friend*, a *Lifetime Friend*, a *Friend in Need*, or a *Warm Friend*. Anyone who contributed less than $25 was, by implication, a *Fair Weather Friend*, but who could send so little? A deed to his share of nesting sites would be sent immediately upon receipt of the appropriate check.

He ate his second pot pie without tasting it and had another angel tit and thought about his degree of friendship with the eagle.

It was considerable, he thought. He wanted those eagles of his to have open country around their nests, fish in their waters, silence in their skies, and nothing but Nature's own debris on their forest floors. He wanted them to thrive, as nobility ought to thrive everywhere.

It was ridiculous, he knew, to fall for the word "perpetual". But he had never made such a gesture before, and surely everyone ought to gamble on eternity at least once. He wrote the check, pleased to be a man of sufficient substance to buy a block of something as primitive and enduring as eagle-inhabited shoreline. That a portion of his own nest egg should cradle the nest eggs of his favorite bird gratified him. He slept very well that night, better than he had in weeks.

The next morning the supervisor came by. "Isn't Plum going with you next month?" he asked. "Jim's trying to talk her into going to Mexico for a bullfight."

Mr. Liveright's shoulder jumped and his lip curled in an angry smile at the loose mention of Plum. "She wouldn't like bullfights," he said, knowing he was wrong. "Of course she's going with me," he added, as the supervisor walked away. "We've had that vacation planned since the first of the year." He thought about possibilities. Maybe he wouldn't come back. This place was almost more than a man could stand. Maybe he and Plum could use his vacation to find a place he could transfer to where work was honorable and letter carriers respected, where a man could enjoy a high station in life by doing well a job that needed doing. "And maybe we won't come back," he called.

"Let me know in writing," came back the bored voice of the supervisor.

That evening, with Plum at the restaurant, Mr. Liveright astonished himself by saying, "I don't like being stood up."

"What do you mean stood up?" Plum's eyes darted around the restaurant.

"Last night. We had a date." His shoulder hopped with misery. "You invited me to dinner."

"Oh, that," she said. "That wasn't a real date. I distinctly remember changing it and saying I'd see you Tuesday."

"I suppose you were out with Jim."

"It's none of your business where I was," she said frostily. "You don't own me. I've been through enough of that for a lifetime." He must have touched a sore spot. "And stop twitching! You know I hate public displays!"

He apologized, trying valiantly to control his movements, and changed the subject. He pulled out a brochure and unfolded it for her. "I haven't been on a real trip since Jess died," he said. "I've been thinking about going to Alaska."

"Oh? When?"

"Last three weeks in July. On our vacation."

"But Seaton, you haven't said word one about vacation since

January," she said. "I went ahead and made my own plans. There's no way I can be gone for three weeks."

"I haven't invited you yet," he interrupted.

"...I've filled the summer up so full I'm going to be run ragged," she chided herself.

But she hastened to encourage him to go alone. He needed some time to himself, didn't he, to think and to plan his course for the next twenty or so years. Why not take his last adult years as seriously as he had taken his first. With his interest in eagles, Alaska would be the perfect place for a vision quest.

They discussed it further later in the evening over warm, expensive orange drink, during the intermission of a Springtime Series Concert. Plum's eyes kept track of everyone there, even while she planned his trip. He would fly to Nome, she said, and rent a vehicle from there: dog sled, maybe, though they probably didn't use dog sleds in the summer. A boat, or a bush plane. He could chew blubber for energy; what did he think God had helped him keep his teeth for, anyway? He might have enjoyed listening to these outrageous suggestions if thoughts of her prior commitments hadn't intruded. But visions of bullfights in Mexico angered him far past the hot stage into the numb, and before the intermission was over, he was wrapped in a chilly distance. It was too bad she couldn't go with him, he told her formally, but he agreed that they should have some time apart. He wasn't going to fly to Nome, don't be ridiculous, but he might drive to Seattle and take a ferry up to Alaska so that he could look over the shoreline. He wasn't going to be lonely, oh no, not with all the single women between here and Juneau. He remembered his eagle brochure and thought of cold water and Sitka spruce. He wondered if those nesting sites he had bought were accessible by boat. When the intermission was over, he was faraway north and cold. They went back to their seats and Plum reached for his hand, but he kept his mental distance – as though he were three seats away.

His chill got him through the rest of spring, almost as though preparing him for a northern summer. Someone else spaded Plum's garden, someone else put up her screens and sprayed her apple tree. Let someone else do the work, he thought; let the one who would

reap the harvest till the soil. Not that he would stop seeing her completely, only that he would back off to where he could see her more
analytically.

She was an adventure, the opposite of somebody's wife. Everyone
had trouble with his wife sooner or later. If she didn't die on him, she
had a nervous breakdown or colitis or she got shrewish or had an affair with some bearded creep who stood for all the wrong things or
she drank sherry out of bottles she kept in the laundry hamper —
thank goodness Jessica had had the good grace to die instead of hu-
miliating him with any of these indiscretions, God rest her soul.
Plum capitalized on these troubles; all the disillusioned husbands
and ex-husbands and widowers found solace and rejuvenation in her.
Long lines of them, he thought. Damn that woman!

He stayed largely away from her so as not to fall back in her net
and spent his time making lists and shopping for what he would need
during he trip. He wrote to Chambers of Commerce and worked on
his car. At the last minute he unplugged everything and gave his cat
to the little girl next door. He locked up, finally, on the tenth of July.

The phone rang just as he closed the door. He let it ring, then decided to answer it.

"I know you're leaving today, Seaton, and I won't keep you, but
have a really good time! Why don't you give me your itinerary so I
can write you now and then?"

His insides shook and his voice was a monotone, but a grin spread
over his face as he told here where he was going.

"Be sure to bring me something pretty," she said.

Pleased in spite of himself he answered, "I'll think about it."
When he hung up and went out the door again, his grin was still
there. She did care! And he was on his way to Alaska! But damn her
for still being able to make the sun shine on him!

The sun shone very little during the first leg of his journey. Mist
and drizzle kept his windshield wipers fanning through Illinois and
Iowa. He drove in his own bubble of isolation; the cars that approached or passed him were ghostly vehicles without human dri-
vers; the farmhouses were uninhabited, no wash on the line, no
chickens in the barnyard. On the outskirts of Council Bluffs the rain

made a tinny noise on the roof of his old-fashioned tourist cabin, where he slept and ate frugally, with creatures that came from under the cracked linoleum, as is fitting for a man who puts his money into nest eggs instead of traveling first class. It sprinkled and showered through Nebraska, causing static in the music on the Omaha stations, and finally all the road grime was washed off his car by a cloudburst as he drove into Cheyenne, where the frontier really begins.

He found another cheap motel, saving his money for better things, then left the car and walked, bright orange in his poncho, along the main street. The rain was letting up and he stopped to look at the window displays: tooled leather boots and belts, fringed leggings, string ties, turquoise jewelry, cowboy hats, moccasins. He dropped in a store now and then for a closer look, but unable, because of the sheer volume of merchandise, to discriminate between treasure and junk, he bought only a packet of post cards. When he came to the end of the business section, he crossed the street and walked back down the other side, feeling lonely for the first time since leaving home.

Summer days last so late when a person is alone. Who is it that daylight is saved for? Not for him. The rain had darkened the sky earlier, but now that it had slowed back down to a leak here and there, the sun was coming back out. What did a man do this time of evening when he had no home to go to?

Nostalgia for the years of his marriage to Jessica, his little home fire, washed over him. She hadn't been perfect, but who was? She was a comfortable woman and had made him a comfortable home. He missed her. He felt a poignant urge to write her a post card. "Dear Jess," it would say, "I'm at the edge of the frontier and I miss you. Could you send me a thought?"

Her answer came to him immediately: "Dear Seaton: By all means cross that edge! Love, Jess."

He laughed aloud. Good old Jess. He went into the Branding Iron and had a char-broiled steak. When he had eaten and was back outside, the rain still fell intermittently, making it necessary for him to wear the poncho whose orange glow cast a bright reflection in the windows. This conspicuous shape looked strange, unlike himself — a bird in new plumage. A harbinger, he thought, a mythical bird with orange plumage and a compelling song. He spread his arms slightly to give the harbinger wings.

In the next window he saw a display of western wear for women: soft suede boots that laced to the knee, jewelry, and, draped softly on the stand, a white squaw dress in a delicate, crinkly fabric, the skirt and sleeves edged with rows and rows of silver braid. He went inside.

"I'd like to see the dress in the window," he told the saleswoman. He knew he would find no better gift to take Plum. She never got her fill of dresses.

"What size?"

His eyes measured her. "About your size."

She brought the dress and held it up to herself. "I think this is the prettiest one we carry," she said, spreading the full skirt wide.

She was a good-looking woman. The dress suited her perfectly. He wondered if she knew where things were happening in Cheyenne. Then he noticed the wide wedding ring. "How much is it?" he asked. Under the poncho he felt his shoulder hopping. Even before the woman named the price, he had decided to buy it.

At the desk the dress was wrapped in blue tissue and laid carefully in a box. He watched. Just before she closed the box, the saleswoman asked, "Anything else?"

He glanced around the store and started to shake his head, then stopped. A jewelry display had caught his eye. "Let me look over here a minute."

She followed him. "These are for men" she said, "but I suppose a woman could wear one if she wanted to."

Jewelry for men. Mr. Liveright had never worn any jewelry except a watch – not even cuff links, not even a wedding band. Yet these necklaces fascinated him. He picked out a silver chain with a thunderbird pendant.

"You'd be surprised how many men wear these," she said.

By this time his breathing was shallow and he felt light. "I'll take it."

Back at the desk the woman started to put the necklace in the box with Plum's dress. "Would you like these sent?"

"No," he answered quickly. "I'll take them with me. And you can leave the thunderbird out. I'll wear it."

She looked up and smiled at him. "Oh," she said. "I thought you were buying it for the lady."

Embarrassed, he struggled with his poncho, tucking the necklace inside.

"There's a mirror," she told him. "Wouldn't you like to see how it looks?"

"I know how it looks," he said hurriedly. He felt himself flush and picked up his package to go.

Outside he put the package under his poncho to protect it from the scattered raindrops. He saw himself reflected again, but now the image had changed to that of a pregnant harbinger about to lay a rectangular egg.

When he was almost back to the motel, he noticed that his shoulder was jerking again, and not only that but his vacation lightheartedness had vanished as well. He felt down in the dumps and his lips were stretched tight across his teeth. It felt almost as though something had happened to return him to his rut.

He stopped short on the sidewalk. "She wouldn't wear it," he said out loud. "I'm a fool to think she would." And he turned around and went back to the store.

"Look," he said. "I'm sorry to trouble you, but I'd like to return this." He laid the box on the desk.

"Oh, that's too bad," exclaimed the saleswoman. "Did you want a different color? Maybe the white wouldn't suit her."

"No," he said. "She wouldn't wear a squaw dress no matter what color it was. It's not her style." He signed the return slip and took his money with great relief.

"You're not returning the necklace too?"

"I'm not returning the necklace." He smiled broadly. His shoulders were square and quiet.

Back at the motel he lit the heater to take off the chill and went to bed, not even bothering to remove the chenille spread, sleeping under the blowsy roses like Pan in a meadow. The thunderbird was hard on his chest. He dreamed of eagles.

.∧.∨.∧.∨.∧

Pastures White with Clover

Every night at bedtime, after the nurse has dried Azure and tried to quiet Indigo and given Cobalt her morphine, I repeat to myself instead of a prayer this reassuring definition learned long ago:

"Not dependent on food from the soil, a bromeliad is a free plant living on nothing at all: sunshine, dew, wind — its soul nourished by the music of spider webs vibrating in its leaves. The pineapple is a bromeliad; so are the air ferns. So is the *Vriesea imperialis*, tall as a man, anchored for balance in sand and filled with twelve gallons of rainwater that supports algae, plankton, wigglers, and a few small fishes — a magnificent, spike-leaved plant that harbors life within."

I am a *Vriesea imperialis*.

For years I have been keeping this incongruity to myself. I do not wish others to turn aside, embarrassed. The person they see now with the necklace of chins, the cobwebs of hair, the legs keg-like with dropsy is an accident. They might laugh at the disparity between my body and my self but their bodies are accidents too and they will someday be in a nursing home, just as I am, too frightened to escape the wheelchair and too restless to endure it. They too will cling to a chosen self.

One must do so, to avoid becoming like the rest. Who could bear to be an Azure, whose only individuality is her odor, or an Indigo, now and forever screeching to die in such a repellant voice that she puts off Death himself? I hear her every time I wheel past our room in my rounds of the Home; today her "Owww" is pitched a little higher than usual.

When I was a girl, choices of identity were limited. My female family members were either the caretakers or the cared-for — either earth around roots or plants rooted in earth. Not one of them simply stood on her own two feet. They were clay, humus, clod, clot — or they were fir, fern or pine. There wasn't a mountain goat in the bunch, and I am the only bromeliad to come from the family. My sister was a Venus flytrap aiming to become a shark, but she died young, God rest her soul.

My spiky leaves, my fishes, my anchoring roots like toes curled in the sand: this comfortable identity becomes all the more precious as other values disappear: home, health, friends, and now, worst of all losses, the mental acuity that gave my character its bite.

It's true — my mind is slipping — one blood vessel at a time; I feel a ping in my head and the date of my husband's death is gone. A ping, a blank spot, a chapter gone — and sometimes the index altered so that I don't even miss what I've lost.

But I'll not dwell on that. I'm far more acute than anyone else here. Wasn't I picked over Rainbow to be the Girl Scout Grandmother? There has to be a reason. It's because one's chosen identity dictates one's development and behavior. Sister Flytrap wouldn't have been picked as a Grandmother either.

It does seem, however, that my being here amongst the caretakers and the cared-for is an uncomfortable irony. I do not fit, yet this is the place for me. Actually, I belong…. Well, there hasn't really been a place designed yet that would suit me.

The physical environment, for instance, is depressing: wipe-clean furniture in the lounge, non-slip floors and guard rails, a sling-and-hoist to ease the helpless into the bath, the odor of air freshener chasing the odor of urine.

And the intellectual environment is even worse. Our nurses, always promoting a facade of cheerfulness, use on us, their elders, that tone of cajoling enthusiasm used on children. "Let's have our bath now, dearie," they say, or worse, "Let's sit on the potty." No one here objects; these old women want to be treated like children; they yearn only to be taken care of.

Except me. I am not like the others. I am a *Vriesea imperialis* with a touch of the majestic. Even so, this is the right place for me. We were agreed on that.

In a progressive nursing home there are, in addition to nurses and janitors, resource people who come to teach yoga and crafts and music appreciation, and to provide inspirational messages.

There was an inspirational message at two o'clock yesterday. I try very hard to remember day and time of day, though I'm afraid the date of my husband's death is gone forever. The only date I'm sure of is 1066.

Yesterday's inspiration came from a middle-aged, altruistic matron like I used to be. She was doing a good work between the beauty shop and the dressmaker's. You could smell the hair spray, anticipate the pins and chalk.

Her message, "Every life is a story," was told in the tone of voice usually reserved for children. She elaborated on her theme at some length. I don't recall what else she said, because her opening statement, "Every life is a story," spoken in that false-cheer tone inspired me so much I didn't need to hear any more.

I was inspired to challenge her. I argued that a story is not well thought of unless it has a plot involving cause and effect, while in my life there have been only effects without causes. She assured me, with bird-like noddings of her lacquered head, that nowadays a story without a plot is considered the very best kind.

"You ought to write your story down," she said. "It could provide inspiration for others." She didn't mention who the others might be.

But this warrants consideration, for never has a less plotted life been lived. Never has there been a more perfect story. And when I get it written, the pings in my head won't matter so much. I'll have my facts on paper.

I told the lady that my story would consist of: a) characters; b) occasional happenings that do not contribute to a plot; and c) a pearl of wisdom. The lady said the pearl of wisdom is also out of style, but I cannot accept that. Wisdom is my strong point; my story's greatest asset will be the pearl. It would be false modesty for me to hold it back.

The hair-sprayed lady took an interest in me, asking about what she called my history. I assured her that I was here by choice and that even a college graduate could end up in a nursing home. At this, her face closed off and she cut our conversation short saying she had to run to keep her appointment with the dressmaker.

They all take an interest in me. I am the star patient here, and in spite of my decline, the most mentally acute. There is another who considers herself the star, but she is mistaken. She must think that knitting colorful afghans makes her a colorful person. I cater to her, call her "Rainbow" to match her knitting though I think of her as a scaly gray. She does not come to hear inspirational messages. She thinks she's too good. I, on the other hand, attend such functions so as to continue my lifetime of good works. The messengers need at least one person in the audience who doesn't let her mouth hang open.

I always tell visitors I am in the Home by choice. They never know how to respond. No one has ever asked me what the alternatives were. Nor has anyone ever asked me by *whose* choice I'm here.

This is something I shall put into my story. Since, as a result of that choice, nothing happens – day after day, around here nothing ever happens – putting it in would not taint the story with cause and effect.

An example of an occurrence that does not have cause or effect is the appearance every so often of a truck bearing the words, "A. J. Lofty, Dealer in Hides, Bones, and Grease." With a plot I might make something of A. J. Lofty's visits, say perhaps that he provides us with a useful service, taking away those who cannot afford funerals and are so decrepit that science won't accept the bodies. But it wouldn't be true and everyone would know it, because one of the Home's well-advertised attractions is a funeral included in the room rate.

Kin can be notified of the funeral if so stipulated in the contract. It costs a little more, but some of them want it.

In my case there are no kin. My husband is dead; the date and year have slipped my mind. I came to the Home when he died. His estate provided that the Home take care of me right through the funeral.

My one worry is this: when my time comes, no one will notify my Own True Love. He will phone me, as he does every day; the phone

I keep wrapped in a blanket and hidden under my bed will ring and ring and ring. It will be found and silenced, and the operator will tell him he has reached a disconnected number. The thought of being a disconnected number so disturbs me that I have considered making friends with someone who could be trusted to notify him. But no one here can be trusted. I will simply have to out live him.

Perhaps it sounds strange that I keep my phone wrapped and hidden, but anyone who lived in the Home would understand. Some of these people would think nothing of answering my phone and saying something outrageous to my love. Since I spend most of my time wheeling around and around our quadrangle of halls, I have to take precautions.

My roommates wouldn't answer my phone, of course, not one of the three could get the phone out from under my bed, which is why I keep it there.

One of my roommates is Indigo, who is now bawling – snuffling and whimpering and wanting to die – loudly – and how I wish she would! But she's the kind who will probably outlast us all. Indigo is a hothouse plant.

In the bed by the window is Azure. No one knows anything about her except the way she smells. She never moves or speaks; she stares out the window worshipping the sky in a catatonic ecstasy.

The third one, Cobalt, is a favorite around here. The nurses all pet her and she has visitors every day – but she will be gone soon. Her already wasted body shrinks further with every tasteless meal. Cobalt is envied. Indigo drinks out of her glass and licks the rim, hoping cancer is contagious.

One can easily understand why I wheel myself around and around the halls, staying in my room only to sleep or dress or use the telephone.

It was thoughtful of my husband to provide for a telephone in my contract. I'm the only person here who has one. I use it mostly for talking with my Own True Love but also for making business calls. I call the bank, for instance, and ask for advice about investing a hundred dollars, or I call the dog pound and report a pack of noisy dogs. I call the radio station to request my favorite songs and the medical service that will play recordings about any disease you can think of

from headache to athletes foot, with liver and hemorrhoids in between. You can get crisis advice if you threaten suicide, and jokes and
even prayers on the phone, though I boycott Dial-a-Prayer. The Lord
is deaf.

But now that I have a story to compose, one that will be an inspiration to others, I will be too busy to make my business calls.

I will of course continue to answer my love's calls, for he needs
the companionship. We cannot see each other; he does not go out
much, though he does get around well enough with a walker to live
alone in a small house he says is not far from here.

He urges me to leave the Home and live with him just as he used
to urge me to leave my husband and run away with him. "Come with
me, my little *Vriesea imperialis*," he would say, "with your algae and
your wigglers and your few small fishes. Come away and be my Own
True Love, my Otl. We belong together."

But I always answered no. "I cannot do it," I would say. "I have a
good marriage. My husband is the sand around my roots, he is my
anchor. Without the anchoring sand, I would topple." Sometimes I
added, "And don't be ridiculous. It's an illusion to 'belong together.'
You can warm my inner fires and keep my fishes healthy. But I cannot run away with you."

He would counter my refusals. He would say, "One day the rains
will come and wash away the anchoring sands and you will topple re-
gretting that we are not together, in spite of the fact that belonging together is an illusion."

It was his correct description of my identity that tempted me most
sorely. One's own name is never spoken; no one can possibly know it.

For that reason I should have gone with him.

For now when my Own True Love phones, he adjusts his hearing
aid to "telephone" and heaves words at me with air from the stomach. His voice is a wreck; there is none of the old stentorian power
that characterized it before the surgery. The word I hear most clearly
is "Otl," pronounced "oh'tl," which he has always called me. It
sounds like a dove's coo and comes though very well on air from the
stomach. On the phone each day he gives me erotic messages which,
considering his age, can hardly be taken seriously. He tells me I am

a ripe red peach in his hand, he is opening me, splitting me, sucking the juice. He tells me he is a hungry bird that pecks the peach until the seed comes out. This kind of mixed metaphor is interspersed with "Otl, my Otl, oh" that sounds like a dove in the rain getting soaked. I will never be too busy with my story for him.

I think perhaps my life's story will be about names. Thus I will introduce each character by name as the color she would be if she were a color. We need colors around here, reds and yellows. But blues predominate, and grays. And women.

There are no men here. Men are sometimes brought in but they die immediately. The last one, Puce, lived long enough to ask each of the women if he mightn't come into her bed and make her happy, exposing himself to anyone who didn't turn away fast enough. After being ignored by all, he went into a decline and died.

The only man to survive here is the administrator. I call him "Whitewash," which fits him to perfection.

Whitewash, who does not deign to eat our food, folds his hands and prays piously before our dinner, filling in the Almighty on our complaints and childishness, asking the Almighty to forgive us, reminding Him to bestow upon us gratefulness for the care and security we receive through His grace, Amen.

I used to follow Whitewash's prayer with an extemporaneous one of my own. I would echo the "Amen!" loudly, then ask the Almighty not to forgive but to punish Whitewash for refusing to acknowledge the realities of old age and death – he closes all our doors when someone dies and the body has to be carried through the halls – while insisting that we attend his classes in Reality Therapy where we learn what day it is. But instead of punishing Whitewash for his cover-ups, the Almighty, night after night, forgave him. I have given up petitioning the Lord. He is deaf.

At dinner time everyone who can be moved is coaxed or dragged or wheeled to the dining room. Whitewash's orders. The few who are on special diet are brought trays; the rest of us eat family style.

At the family style tables the food is salt-free, sugarless and low in cholesterol. We get no raw fruits or vegetables, no meats that require chewing, nothing greasy or gassy, nothing that will loosen the bowels

— or bind them. To forestall allergic reactions, they serve no milk or chocolate, no wheat or nuts. And for reasons unexplained they give us no seeds, spices, seasonings, skins, or savory tidbits. The little that's left — mashed potatoes, usually — is served lukewarm so that the ones who put their heads down to sleep won't burn themselves.

I asked Whitewash what the people on special diet got to eat.

"At the Home," he answered, "a person who is considered a candidate for 'special diet' can eat anything." How could he possibly provide security and care for the rest of us, he asked, if he took any chances on giving us food that might make us sick?

Some discreet questioning jogged my memory to the fact that the contracts can be drawn "special diet" for an additional fee.

My husband, bless his heart, did not approve of frills, nor did I; our life together was austere at all times. Why he thought the phone would be a necessity for me I neither knew nor questioned. Maybe it was free; he worked all his life for the telephone company. But special diet was another matter, quite needless, like a bed near the window or a room near the toilet. At the time we drew up the contract I was so attracted to ascetic virtue that I wouldn't have dared to ask for any luxury to be included or that I be left some money to use as I thought best. It never entered my mind to question his wisdom. He had, after all, taken good care of me.

As far as where the rest of the money went — and there must have been more, because we certainly never wasted anything on frills — we always chewed half a stick of gum and used half a paper napkin — what became of the rest of it I never knew, or if I did, I've misplaced the memory. I came here the day he died, I know that, but my head's been pinging ever since and I can't remember the decade, let alone the date. The only date I have firmly in mind is 1066, and no one will tell me what happened on that day.

Which reminds me that I really should place my story in a time setting. I think I'll take the luxury of decreeing that the time be now, a little later than then, with soon coming up.

But right now coming up is Rainbow, interrupting my thoughts, putting an end to my story. I can't possibly write with her around.

Rainbow has a motorized wheel chair that chugs along at one slow speed. In spite of her motor, she can't go as fast as I can. She knits a continuous afghan in many colors, knitting even while her chair moves, guiding it with her elbow, never wasting a minute.

"Good afternoon, Thornapple," she says heartily, showing the sharp teeth she prizes so highly. Rainbow finds it amusing to name people as the plants she says they would be if they were plants. She read about the game in a Growth book. She's very trendy.

"Did you watch the talk show on TV last night?" she asks. I never listen to TV. She knows that. "No," I answer. "I never listen to TV."

"That's a mistake, Thornapple," she says with authority. "You can't keep up with what's going on in the world unless you watch TV."

I keep my own counsel and think my own thoughts.

"One of those men on the talk show said a new world is coming," she continues. "He said that in the days to come food and space will be so limited that only the people who are useful will be allowed food and space." Rainbow looks up from her afghan and peers at me through her rimless, old-lady spectacles. "What do you think of that, Thornapple?"

I think I would like to hit her but I won't. The one who hits is always to blame; the one who provokes is innocent. Rainbow is my little sister all over again. She's exactly what Sister Flytrap would have been at this age if she'd lived, bless her heart, right down to the teeth. Sister Flytrap was a biter, but she never left marks, and, as my mother said, I always loved her dearly.

"It will be decided by computer," Rainbow goes on. "The person who makes a contribution will be allowed to eat and occupy space."

"Is that so?" I say politely. "And how is this marvelous computer going to compute contributions?"

"By the long term benefit to humankind," she says, knitting faster. Rainbow sells afghans. She bought her own way into the Home and with the money she makes she purchases herself such frills as motorized wheel chairs. Each time she sells an afghan she goes on special diet for a while.

"Surely you can't be worried about this," I say.

"Oh, but I can," she answers. "Supporting oneself won't count as a contribution."

"You don't say!" She's lorded it over the rest of us for years about the worthiness of standing on one's own two feet.

Rainbow continues. "On the talk show it was said that there won't be enough food or space left for all the people, even, who are able to support themselves. Society will have to decide which ones it will allow to have the jobs."

"You shouldn't listen to so much TV," I tell her. "It's bad for your system."

She ignores me. "Society now feels that self-support is to an individual's credit," she said, "but why should the individual derive wealth and status from a job that society has handed him?"

Rainbow may not be the star of the Home, but she's the star of the Reality Therapy class. She always seems to sense what they're going to call "reality" from one day to the next, and she'll fall for it even if it's to her disadvantage, like this new thing on the TV.

"The old idea that everyone who wants to can get ahead has a flaw in it. *Anyone* can," she says with emphasis, "but not *everyone*. Take the Kentucky Derby," she goes on. "*Any* horse at the starting gate might win, but…"

"Rainbow," I interrupt, "there's Communism lurking in the dust balls under your bed."

Though I berate her I am distressed. If this new order comes to pass, the aged will be the first to go. They'll begin by saying we are vegetables and no longer human. They'll find something to call us to make it okay to quit feeding us. The Home seems much less safe to me now. What's a contract, anyway, in times like that?

Rainbow is still talking. "…more like Calvinism than Communism," she says. "People used to strive to please God, and God decided who got His grace and the life everlasting. Now they'll have to strive to benefit mankind and the computer will decide who is successful and gets the next meal." Rainbow sounds agitated. "Under Communism people who weren't enemies of the state got to eat. Now only the ones who make a contribution will get to. This will eliminate the hungry mouths that are connected only to a gut; a brain and hands will have to be connected as well from now on, but…" Her voice peters out.

My hands finger each other, touch the nails and knuckles. They feel wrinkled and dry and old and useless. They feel unconnected to anything. I don't want to think about my brain or about my situation.

Rainbow motors away slowly, the finished end of her afghan picking up lint from the hall floor. "I'd better tell the others," she says. She enjoys being the bearer of this kind of news.

"Why bother?" I call after her. "Does the gardener tell his beets and cucumbers that they are about to be pulled and pickled?"

"If I were you, Thornapple, I would stop being so poisonous!" she exclaims, still moving away.

Suddenly I notice how angry I am. "You don't know it," I shout, "but I am going to write a story with a pearl of wisdom in it that will inspire others and be my contribution and I will go on special diet while you subsist on afghan stew!"

"Now, Thornapple!" she says. "I wouldn't work up an appetite if I were you. No one cares for your story or your pearl of wisdom. There is already more wisdom around than anyone can possibly use. There's a pearl choker on every neck. I'd draw in my belt if I were you, Thornapple!" She sounds victorious, just like my sister, who used to crow when I'd be whipped.

"Don't call me 'Thornapple'," I shout. "That's not my name!" I have tolerated her sloppy misnomer for too long already.

"You don't call me by my right name either," she answers. And she chugs away toward my room where Cobalt lies dying and Azure gazes at the sky and Indigo howls at her own longevity.

Everything's changing with indecent speed. I feel a ping in my head; a blood vessel bursts. I feel the sands slipping away from my roots; my fishes swim away.

I wheel after Rainbow. When I catch up, I say, menacing her with a spiky stare, "Don't you dare tell Cobalt." Someone has to protect the helpless. It's better to die of cancer than of uselessness.

"I don't know who you mean by 'Cobalt'," she answers in her smug, busybody way, from behind her impregnable fence of teeth.

I am frustrated in the extreme. I have called the poor thing "Cobalt" for so long I can't remember her given name. Rainbow chugs off again while I am thinking and is spared violence – I could ram her chair with my own, and don't think I wouldn't do it – only because I hear the muffled ringing of my telephone. I head for my room, blocking Rainbow. She decides wisely to go somewhere else.

It will be my Own True Love, once blond and handsome, calling to ask me to run away with him. This time I will go. Perhaps together we can make a contribution and benefit mankind. I pull the phone out from under the bed and unwrap it.

"Otl?" he asks, his breath whistling in a duet with Indigo, who is wailing as usual. "Is this my Otl speaking?"

I can hardly hear him because of the noise Indigo makes. "Shhh!" I hiss at her; then, "My fishes are gone!" I cry into the phone.

"I'm glad to hear it," he says. "If the dishes are done, you can come to me. It isn't far."

His hearing aid must be set for "speech" instead of "telephone." This happens when he wants to make a speech instead of listen. And I want to tell him I'm ready. Always a conflict.

"Set that thing for 'telephone'," I scream at him.

But he is well into his speech. "Go out the front door and down the walk," he says patiently. Just as if I didn't know how to do anything right. "When you come to the street, turn left, now mind you, toward the edge of town where the lake is. Keep going that way and I'll meet you." There is a silence. He is waiting for my answer.

While I try to think how to phrase my desire to come to him, he says, "Hold on while I adjust this thing."

I calculate how long the adjustment will take, then I plunge into my answer. "Yes," I say, "I want to come to you now but I'm afraid. How am I going to get up and down curbs?" I ask, beginning to wonder if the plan is even possible.

When he doesn't answer, I continue, "Won't that look silly? They'll take me out of the nursing home and put me in the loony bin."

"Don't worry," he gasps, sounding as though he tried to speak on the end of an air gulp. "The loony bin has gotten so full that all the nuts are staying in the trees." He cackles at his pathetic joke, the cackle a cruel caricature of the booming laugh he used to have, the joke all that's left of his wit.

But he is still struggling to talk. "If we're afraid of looking silly, we're never going to be together, not even for a few minutes." There is a piercing noise as his hearing aid squeals.

"I'll leave now," he says. "You come in my direction and I'll come in yours, and pretty soon we'll meet."

"And what if we don't?" I cry. I'm afraid to think of what will happen to me in the streets alone.

There is a silence. "We will if you follow my instructions," he says, finally. He does not elaborate.

The plan seems less and less feasible. "I am busy," I say. "I am too busy to meet you." I'd better stay where I am. This is the right place for me.

He is angry. "You've used that excuse too often!" he shouts. "You are not too busy. You told me the dishes are done!"

"I am busy indeed," I answer, happy that I have remembered. "And not washing dishes, either. They have dishwashers here. I am busy composing a story that has a pearl of wisdom in it that is so valuable that it will be my contribution."

Air is gulped. "What on earth are you talking about?" he wheezes.

That's right; he doesn't listen to TV either. He doesn't even own a set.

"Why are you gabbling about a curly wishbone at a time like this?"

"Pearl of wisdom," I enunciate, trying to be patient. "It's that when one's name is called, one must go," I say. I am embarrassed; the pearl has not yet been stated in such a direct way. It sounds flawed and small without the velvet cushion of the story cradling it.

Through the phone comes a long sigh. "I have been calling your name for thirty-seven years," he whispers. "And you haven't come. No one will eat the soup if the cook's afraid to taste it."

He is right, of course. Maybe that wasn't the pearl after all. It's hard to remember details when you're my age. I question him again. "How did you know my name?" I am stalling, of course. It is only a matter of time, how, until I go to meet him. Poor old man, he'll be out on the street looking for me. No telling what will happen to him. Before he can answer the first question, I ask another. "And why are you so sure we ought to be together?"

"I learned the name you call yourself by eavesdropping," he says defiantly. "You were talking to yourself, extremely angry. You were saying, 'I'm *not* a bramble bush, I'm *not* a barrel cactus, I'm *not* a haw tree or a jimsonweed, I'm a *Vriesea imperialis* with twelve gallons of water supporting algae, wigglers, and a few small fishes! I have life within me that must be sustained!' You sounded so certain that I called you that to see what would happen."

And with my fishes and the sand around my roots, my belief in the power of love's magic streams away. Eavesdropping.

But he is still speaking. "No one knows another person's name," he says. "No one even knows his own name." He sounds very tired.

I shall wear him out. He mustn't go into the street. The dangers there...

"Why are you so dedicated to our being together?"

"One has to be dedicated to something," he says, "or one crumbles. I'm coming your way," the dry old voice goes on. "I'll meet you soon."

There is one thing I must tell him first. "I'm not a ripe red peach any longer," I say. "I've grown old. I have false teeth and swollen legs."

But he has hung up and I hear the dial tone buzzing in my ear. It doesn't quite drown out Indigo, who is tuning up again.

I pack my things in a large purse, hurrying. If that woman doesn't hush, I'll lose my mind, what little is left of it. What a relief it's going to be to get away from her!

Not many things, just the necessities. Elastic stockings, lemon drops, eau de cologne, denture cleanser. Poor old fellow, he needs someone to look after him.

I ought to dress up. My Girl Scout Grandmother outfit. It'll have to do; it's all I've got. Up out of the wheel chair, old lady! Hang on to the bedpost. Get your glad rags on.

It's a good thing these scarecrows in here are too far gone to notice me and call anyone. If the nurses knew what I was doing... Arms in the armholes, there now, head in the neck, easy. I'd better mention this weakness in my arms to the doctor next time he comes.

There, I'm ready. Back into the wheel chair, purse on lap. I feel as though I'm forgetting something important, but then I always feel that way. I'm always right, too.

At Cobalt's bed I stop. "Goodbye, Cobalt," I whisper.

She wakes up looking startled. "Is it my time?" she asks. "Have they called the priest?" She rolls her eyes back in her head, then closes them tight and says, "Goodbye," very faintly. There's not much use explaining. I pat her hand and leave before the tear in my eye runs down my face. I turn left down the hall, as my Own True Love instructed.

At the nurses' station the nurse on duty speaks to me in that voice that's used on children, "And where are you going, young lady, all dressed up fit to kill?"

I loiter for a moment and make small talk. "It's such a nice spring day I thought I'd go out for a little walk." I laugh deprecatingly to show that I've got enough sense to know I can't walk. "I might drop in on my Girl Scout troop." She won't believe me anyway.

She leans heavily on the counter that encloses the nurses' station. "Speaking of spring," she says significantly, "I heard you got excused from Reality Therapy."

She's right. Yesterday it was, or maybe the day before. The reality lesson was on the season. They told us it was spring and showed us that the calendar we are required to mark off had been turned to the page for May. Their reality of calendars is meant to cover up our reality of fear and sickness and approaching death. Whitewash closes our doors when someone dies. We're not supposed to know.

Just to open a discussion I spoke up. "Spring is the season when violets bloom and young men's fancies turn and it gets warm and people plant gardens," I said. "Are any of you planting a garden?" I asked. "Is it any warmer than usual?" The Home is kept at a stifling eighty degrees year round. "Do those look like violets?" I asked, pointing to the papier-mâché container holding a spray of gladiolus spikes from the funeral home. We always get hand-me-down flowers from funerals; we're the next echelon. By the time I was finished questioning the importance of reality to people in our situation, the others were convinced that it was not spring at all and that someone had tampered with the calendar. The point was missed as usual.

Whitewash told me I was excused from Reality Therapy for the next week.

"C'est la vie," I tell the nurse. "He'll let me back when he sees how confused I am." I allow my laugh to cackle slightly.

She answers with the big laugh of a fat woman and I wheel myself on down the hall. The nurse goes back to her magazine. She knows I won't go anywhere, a silly old thing like me.

Nearer the door, where the corridors join, I see the woman I call Rainbow. Rainbow thinks herself the star of the Home and now that I'm leaving, she can be. She is knitting on a many-colored afghan that drapes over her shoulder and stretches out on the floor behind her and is talking to a ninety-three year old who is alive in name only. I hear a few words, "...the new Calvinism that's coming," and find them irritating. Rainbow is always striving to use the vocabulary of intellectualism. This time she can show off all she likes; the old one won't challenge her.

"Hello," I call out to them, trying to be friendly. "Haven't seen you two lately."

The old one doesn't respond and Rainbow is not friendly. She speaks to me with malice in her voice and a sharp-toothed, hypocritical smile. "How's that marvelous story coming along?" Rainbow is not accountable. Not much left upstairs. She knows I never read stories.

I humor her along, the poor thing. "Fine," I say. One has to be patient with her. But suddenly my patience runs out and I am snapping at her, "You should have ended that afghan and started another one three yards ago!" My wheel chair heads in her direction and runs over the afghan tail. I wheel as fast as I can to the foyer, turn and slip through the door as it closes behind a visitor. I roll down the ramp. There!

Outside it feels chilly. Is it spring or isn't it? I forgot how the decision went. But then I see the line of tulips along the walk and I am sure. That's lucky, because if it's spring, I don't need a coat. In fact, I don't think I own a coat.

At the end of the walk I lean out of my chair and pick a frazzled tulip for my buttonhole. I finger up and down my front but find no place to put it. I tuck the tulip in my hair instead and feel it slide down over my ear. It can take the place of a hat. "In my Easter Bonnet, with all the frills upon it..." It feels festive to be wearing a hat.

Two little girls at the awkward age, wearing what looks like their brothers' hand-me-downs, appear on the street. One of them says, "It's our Grandmother." The other one, who might be pretty with a little fixing up, says, "Hello, Grandmother." I offer each one a lemon drop since they spoke so politely.

"Thank you, Grandmother," they say and hurry off before I can mention that they'd look nice in dresses. But I'm puzzled. I'm sure I have no grandchildren.

I follow them, but slowly, and when we reach the corner I turn while they continue, for I'm afraid to call them back to help me down the curb. They wouldn't intend to, but they might tip me over.

I stop for a moment to get my bearings, then continue, slowly. I seem to be in a residential block. The houses are shabby and the children dirty. Some of them are barefoot. They are playing a game that involves throwing clods of earth at each other. They stare as I pass and I speed up, hoping not to be a target. These children look uncared for, and sure enough, there isn't a caretaker in sight.

At the corner I stop again and notice that I am shivering. It's really quite chilly. I oughtn't to be out without a coat.

On the other side of the street I see a row of shops. I'd like to go in one and get warm. Maybe it would be a candy store. But I'd better wait and find one on this side of the street. There's too much traffic for me to make it across, the way those trucks and cars are speeding. I continue to roll along.

The walk is untidy with twigs and sticks and breaks in the pavement. I avoid the large holes but there are too many small ones to miss them all. Does it break your mother's back to run over a crack in a wheel chair? Probably not, but I try not to take chances. I wouldn't want to hurt Mother. I turn the corner.

Ah, here comes someone. But I'd better not speak. I'm not supposed to speak to strangers. Mother said so. I can look, though, out of the corner of my eye. It's a priest. That's different. "Hello, Father," I say. I'm not Catholic, but it never hurts to speak to a priest. "Hello, Grandmother," he answers. Grandmother? I didn't know I was his grandmother.

And around this corner the shops and houses give way to a low building with a row of windows all along the front. At the curb is a truck marked "A. J. Lofty, Hides, Bones and Grease." It looks familiar but with my memory the way its been lately I can't place it. I hurry past, trying not to breathe, because the truck smells terrible. Near the entrance to the building is a sign, "Sunnyside Nursing Home," and under it a message; "Where life is, there too is hope." But through one of the windows I see a blank withered face that looks as though the sign is mistaken, that there is no hope anywhere.

I feel myself trembling and I wheel as fast as I can past that place. It must be unbearable to be in a nursing home among all those old crones. I don't think I could stand it.

/\/\/\/\/\

Concordia

When Pearce awakened on the Sunday morning, he found himself pressed tightly against Marta's back. Withdrawing slightly, he dozed around the pain in his head. "To sleep," he thought, "and not to dream, that this too solid life be rounded with a charm." He woke up a little more and studied critically what he had just thought. Here he was, his mind filled with a salad of English Department words, while his crazy son was already traveling home on the Greyhound bus. What kind of a father was he?

That was not the worst of it. He had maintained congeniality with the incoming students at the dean's open house last night, listening to the ideas they thought were new: that the past is history (and can be sneered at); the future doesn't exist (and can be ignored); seize the day (and wrestle it to the ground). It had taken quite a few too many drinks to get him through it. His reward for benign restraint was a hangover.

Yesterday Marta had asked him to raise one corner of the mattress while she put a fitted sheet on their son's bed.

"Let him make his own bed," he had exclaimed. "Let him lie in it. He's thirty-two years old, for God's sake. What can I do for a thirty-two year old man who thinks I've had him fired from every job he's ever had, evicted from every room he's ever rented, dumped by every woman he's ever wanted? Who thinks I'm behind his arrest? Tell me, what can I do?" He heard his own voice. It made him stop. He imagined what Marta was thinking.

"You can help me make a nice place for him to come home to," she said. He helped with the bed.

What else could he do for his son? For Marta? What could he do for himself?

Now, awake and in the kitchen, he made a pot of coffee and sat at the table to drink it. Maybe the students are right, he thought. There's something to be said for living in the present.

He considers the uses of the present. In the present, you are a pair of eyes, he thinks. What you see is not connected to your heart, to all the meaning accrued by past events. In the present the questions are simple.

He might practice living in the present. He looks at the table in front of him, notices that the Formica is not really plain blue but has some flecks of white in it. He sees his coffee cup, the cup he brought home from their fifteen days in Mexico. He tries to see it for what it is, a straight-sided mug with a handle so flat to the side that he can't get a finger through it. It has a buff-white background. Purplish-blue zigzag lines decorate the rim and the base. The cup is painted all around with flowers of that same shade of purplish-blue, and in their midst is a single orange daisy that brings on an odd, happy feeling when he looks at it.

He remembers buying the cup for two U.S. dollars in the foothill town of Concordia from the potter himself, his wheel set up in a shaded corner of the yard he shared with a burro, a pig and piglets, a flock of chickens and his wife. The wife ground corn and slapped tortillas for the tourists who came to Concordia in air-conditioned buses with English-speaking guides. Their son, about fifteen, manned the gate and sold his mother's tortillas and his father's pottery.

But all this is past. Consider the daisy on the cup. The potter and his son are history.

Marta came into the kitchen wearing a brown skirt and rose-colored cardigan. "Today's the day," she said. Her hair was freshly curled in a style he hadn't seen recently. When he glanced at it, she said quickly, "It's been a long time. I don't want to look like a stranger."

She poured herself some coffee. "Are you feeling better? You did a lot of groaning in the night."

"I feel fine." It would be yielding to the past to tell her that he had vomited once, twice, taken aspirin and vomited again during the night.

"That was quite a party," she said.

"I don't want to dwell on it."

"I'll bet you don't."

He turned to face away from her. It wasn't the alcohol he regretted; it was his attempt to be jolly with the new students. He certainly hadn't felt jolly. Now, at least, he was acting as much of a horse's ass as he felt. Poor Marta! She didn't deserve this, but he couldn't help it.

"What should we do?" she asked. "Should we take him out to dinner, or do you think he'd like a home cooked meal?"

"Can't you ever think about the present? Must you always be off in the future somewhere?"

"What's the matter with you?" she said. "You're not yourself this morning. You want some herb tea? Maybe the coffee is too much on your stomach."

"I'm more myself than I've ever been in my life."

She reached for his cup. "Here, I'll pour out the dregs and make you some *Stomach Ease*."

"Don't touch that cup," he said and grabbed for it. The cup fell to the floor. He heard it break.

"What's going on?" she asked. "I don't get the point."

He reached down and picked up the crockery pieces and laid them on the table. "The point is to regard the cup," he said. "The point is to stay in the present and look at things from your own eyes. The past is finished, the future doesn't exist, and you can't know what anybody else is seeing anyway."

"Oh," she said.

After a moment she said, "I get it. You're pulling out on me, aren't you? I'm going to have to handle it all."

He didn't answer. When she left the room, he noticed that the cup had broken into three pieces, the orange daisy centered in a V-shaped shard.

The noontime heat in Concordia had been punishing. He had huddled in the shade of whatever building or tree was available and fanned himself with the map in a futile attempt to dry the salty sweat that ran in his eyes. Marta stayed with their tour group, photographed the church, the outdoor furniture factory with its sawyers and lathe operators stripped to the waist, but he had barely glanced at these attractions. Instead, he went back to the shady yard where the potter and his family worked. He leaned on the brick fence. The mother and son talked with each other or with their neighbors. The man worked quietly in the corner of the yard. The man was a good father.

He is now jolted into the present by Marta's return to the kitchen. "You can't do this," she says. "He's your son too. You're as responsible as I am."

Pearce keeps his gaze on the piece of pottery, but he can see her out of the corner of his eye. Will their son know that she has arranged her hair especially for him? Will he care? Will he be kind to her?

She leaves, and soon he hears the door slam and her car pull out of the driveway.

Suddenly he is on his feet. He walks fast to the bedroom where he strips off his pajamas and pulls on jeans and shirt. His bare feet slip into his loafers.

His car is parked on the street. He slides in. He knows which way she would have gone. He knows a faster way. He can get there first.

But after driving to the stoplight, he realizes that she has too much of a start on him. Wouldn't he feel silly tearing up to the Greyhound Station just as they pull away?

So he returns home, parks the car and takes up his contemplation of the cup. History, he thinks. His head hurts.

His wife and son are together now. The bus station is so close, the town so small, the cup so shattered. He wishes he had taken the job at the minor college in the large town instead of the other way around. He might have had a peaceful Concordia with a harmony of family, quiet work in the yard, a vast distance between his home and the bus station.

Is "might have been" present or past? To what use can history be put? Wherein is man responsible?

Pearce is blocked behind a pile up of questions that cannot be answered.

He hears Marta's car. He busies himself with the pieces of pottery, two in his right hand, one in his left. He is just able to hold them to-gether as a whole vessel. The cracks are invisible.

He doesn't look up at first. When he speaks, his son is already in the kitchen. "It's all past history, Son," he says. The zigzag border is what he notices now, the blue-purple lightning around the rim, the storm filling the cup, the cup running over. He tightens his grip on it.

"You're right, Dad." He hears what might be love spilling out in his son's voice.

He sees his wife in the doorway watching their son cross the kitchen toward him. His son is the same as ever, wearing the same jeans and tee shirt he wore at age fifteen, age ten, age five. He hears his wife's sharp breath. History hits him full force. Blood from the cut on his palm trickles down the side of the cup, following the path of the crack, a drop settling in the point of the V.

.\\.\\.\\.\\.

Tearing

The funeral had taken only a few minutes. The minister hadn't known her and didn't pretend he had. She had no family, she said; she came from nowhere. She left nothing but a drawer full of white cotton underwear and other plain and practical garments hung in the nearly bare closet. These were the things she left, and two more: a thin notebook covered in brown cardboard and a demolished eight year-old Ford.

Afterward Mrs. Kesslar made cocoa for the two lodgers back from the funeral. She thickened the cocoa with marshmallows and served sugar wafers, two each, on a plate. She put out paper napkins with crimped edges and moved the plant with its real-looking leaves off the coffee table, making room for the three of them to sit comfortably, stirring their cocoa with wear-sharpened spoons while she read them the notebook triumphantly.

August 19th. I'm here in a new place with the past gone and the future ahead. I brought nothing, no one, with me, nothing to remind me of what I used to be, the roles I used to play. I want the tears to find new channels down my cheeks and the heels of my shoes to run over on the other side. Before I came here, I packed away my past in boxes, sealed and labeled them, and gave them to the Goodwill. Here I can live with no illusions, no memories, no pretenses, deep under my skin where it hurts. I want to write down the steps I take to reach wherever I'm going so that when I get there I can see the path I took. But not the path to here. I have made a terrific jump and landed in a field of clean snow with no footprints behind me. When the snowflake on my hand melts, at that moment I begin to live. Now.

This room is a good place for that kind of living. Nothing here distracts. I can go straight to the heart of things. One window looks out over the neighbor's garbage cans and has a white curtain to cover the view. The other window has no curtain, but no matter — the view is of the park across the street and doesn't need a cover. The chest of drawers is tall and has an extra blanket in the bottom drawer. There is a shelf for books. I didn't bring any books. I can't think with books in the room. The walls are a warm clay color, a sort of pink, and the sunlight makes a glow in the corner. I have one chair, a small table I can use for writing, and a bed that is solid and comfortable, but shabby. One of the bedposts is broken off and lying in the closet waiting to be repaired.

August 22nd. I seem to be the only woman in this rooming house, with the exception of Mrs. Kesslar, who sits all day in a hooded wicker chair fitted out with accessories: foldaway writing arm, gooseneck lamp, inflatable pillow, and a pocket on the side stuffed with every sort of thing; so far I've seen her take out pliers, a bottle of ink, her rent-receipt book, and a cheese sandwich. She tries to talk to me about the other lodgers, three or maybe four men, but since I have no interest in them, I do not listen. I did not come here to get involved with a man.

August 26th. Today I found a job, one that pays enough for me to live but not enough for me to value the living. That is the kind of job to have. A person must live adequately to think, but when he begins to grow attached to the life, through luxury of one kind or another, he starts making sacrifices to preserve it. Aged beef, Fundador in the coffee, silk clothing, horsepower — luxuries that keep him in bondage. Soon even the luxuries themselves must be given up, as they take up time that he must spend earning money to preserve them. Such a person never says no and never means yes. He works evenings and misses the sunset; he works weekends and misses friends. After four months he is lost; he lives only to sacrifice and doesn't even know it. Luxuries are like illusions — they feel so soft and warm that one becomes a slave to them, then has to give them up in order to keep them.

September 2nd. I hadn't counted on being lonely here, but I am. I thought I would welcome having nobody to talk to. I don't really want to know anyone that well, well enough to talk to, but the quietness bothers me, rattling around my room at night, invading my privacy. I walk every evening so that I will be able to sleep without memories; I write a letter to the editor of the newspaper every morning so that I will not become a recluse. There are no people close to me at work, only two women who are so distant that I keep the conversations to a minimum when they approach my desk. It is very lonely here, but that is, after all, what I wanted.

September 8th. I am getting used to my job. I work in a library mending books. I paste transparent strips over tears in the paper and replace worn covers. Sometimes I type out a page, using another copy of the book to find the right words, and paste it in where a whole page has been removed. The missing pages are always exciting, describing scenes of great violence, or difficult seductions. The variety of violence and seduction is amazing. Sometimes two or three pages are missing and then one can always tell that violence and seduction are mixed. I have never encountered a missing page that described a mutual seduction, only the will of one bending the will of the other. Sometimes the woman persuades the man, though usually the man is the pursuer.

I do not read the books in the library, only the missing pages. In this way I get the essence of many books without being hindered by trivia.

September 10th. I brought some paste from the library to repair the bedpost but it doesn't work. The bed's lack of symmetry bothers me, like an interrupted wheel or an unfinished life. A bed should always have four posts. Mrs. Kesslar will not listen when I ask her to make the repair; she says I must be dreaming, that nothing is wrong with the bed.

Today is a day of complaints. The table is too low to fit the chair; I am forced to do my writing in this unsymmetrical bed. I brought some books home from the library to put under the table legs, but then I couldn't resist reading them, a total waste of time. One was by

Henry James. The nearest thing to seduction in it was a long look and there was no violence at all. The pages were intact.

The evening sun fails to brighten the grayness of these walls. It is a drab room, but proper. Gaiety would be more than I could bear now.

September 16th. Something new and happy has entered my life, though I am so unprepared it frightens me. I have fallen in love again, in love with a man in the rooming house, a warm-hearted, sturdy man one can't help loving immediately.

He has been kind to me ever since I arrived, bringing me bits of treasure that he finds while making his rounds — one day an enameled coat button covered with silver filigree, another a yellow pencil with a soft lead. He makes orange juice in the mornings, and if he catches me he insists that I drink a glass with him. When he goes out walking evenings, he often asks me to go with him, though I have always refused. I didn't come here to get involved with a man.

He followed me to the park last night and sat with me while I ate my dinner picnic-style as I always do. We fed the birds together, the birds that waddle up with their thrusting necks and gulp the crumbs from my dinner. He told me of his life, a harder one than mine, and of the reasons he is here. He questioned me and I answered, but I didn't really tell him anything. He speaks in a deep voice that seems to echo through my past and speaks well, leaving silences of the right length.

He has the voice for love and the hands too, hands that know more than he does. I knew I was lost to him. His voice, his hands, the smell of him, the warm, secure man-smell of him were more than I could resist. I went when he asked me to walk into the dark woods with him to a spot off the path where there is a small clearing among the trees and bushes. There, with the night sounds wrapped around us, we undressed and explored each other. The evening stretched out: time for quietness and warm hands, time for whispering and warm bodies, time even for my frozen heart too thaw and my tight legs to loosen.

We returned to our rooms separately so Mrs. Kesslar would have nothing to say. She must not find out about this.

September 22nd. I cannot understand what has happened. My lover has abandoned me. He speaks to me and tips his hat if we meet, but he acts as though nothing took place between us. He no longer brings me treasures; he puts away the orange juice without offering me any. In the evenings he walks alone and avoids the park.

I knocked at his door last night while Mrs. Kesslar was out playing bridge, but he did not answer. Why has this happened. What did I do wrong? Why did I ever allow myself to become soft and waiting, vulnerable? I knew, I knew — why did I do it? And to think it should happen to me, one who knows these things. I thought I had no illusions left.

September 27th. Thank goodness for my work. It helps me forget. I am always very busy. Many people remove pages from library books. It surprises me. Why can't they copy the pages they need the way I do? I wouldn't tear them out and deprive other people. I copy them and bring them here to distract me when the sounds of my lover moving around in his room make me long for him.

September 30th. Today I was almost killed. I was standing on a street corner waiting to cross when a truck loaded with stones rattled close to the sidewalk. One of the stones fell off, missing me by only a few inches. People exclaimed and the policeman made a joke. I pictured myself crushed by the stone and the policeman sweeping me into the sewer, my flattened body disappearing through the mesh.

October 2nd. If I'm to keep this journal at all, I should at least be honest in it. I don't know what came over me when I wrote about my love affair. I must have been writing without knowing what I was saying.

What really happened was quite different. There were no treasures, no button, no orange juice, no walk, no conversation. I was sitting in the park that night reading a seduction page I had copied for my file when the man from the rooming house joined me. Conversation was difficult, as it always had been with him, so to keep things going I showed him the page. He read it and got up abruptly, pulled me to my feet and walked me to the clearing in the woods that I described before. He was agitated and he fumbled with my clothes. I tried to tell him I wasn't that kind of woman, but he didn't listen. He tore my underpants getting them off; he is very strong, much more so than he appears. I was startled more than frightened. After all, he was a man I had seen at the rooming house nearly every day. One can only be truly frightened of a stranger. And besides, what good would it have done to scream? No one believes a woman when she says she has been raped unless the man is a stranger, or black, or wild-eyed.

October 12th. I have avoided even looking at the rapist in this rooming house. He knows his guilt. I stay in my room with the door locked. I do not go to the park.

It isn't that I dislike sex. What I dislike is the indignity of being pushed down and having my clothes torn, being frightened and hurt, being bruised by the sticks and stones under me, being unprepared and thus unable to enjoy it the way that wooden Indian enjoyed it, as if I were no more to him than a hole in the ground.

October 21st. My people are right. They tear out only pages of violence and difficult seductions. There is nothing else. The will of one bending the will of the other. The body of one tearing the body of the other.

October 25th. I am so lonely here. It is almost unbearable. I have considered going back, but that would be even worse. No, I'll never go back. Sometimes I plan to open my door, but when I remember the rapist in this rooming house, I decide to stay lonely and unbruised.

It is better, anyway, than illusion and disappointment. People have the illusion of being together with another person, of being one, of loving. This is foolishness. If a person has need of love, then he isn't worth the loving. He wants it only to make up for the deficiencies in himself, to feed his vanity. And, if he has no deficiencies, then he does not need the loving, does not value it; it is a nuisance to him. I am glad to be here alone where there is no illusion of closeness.

October 28th. It has grown cold here, much colder than it would be at home. And, as my illusions go, I feel the wind more keenly. Soon I will be naked in the elements and will become comfortable with the truth.

November 2nd. I have been struggling with myself. My cloak of illusion is hard to take off. But I am sure that once I know the truth I'll be free and happy.

Perhaps that is what is wrong, the thought of being free and happy. Maybe one cannot be both. Certainly knowing the truth frees one but does not make one happy. But I have no capacity for happiness anyway, knowing what I do of expectation turning to disappointment, eagerness to bitterness, illusion to reality. I'll settle for truth and freedom.

That is why I must change what I wrote about my night in the park. It wasn't truthful. I was making up a pretty story.

Actually, I went to the park that evening because I knew the man would be there at that time. He always attracted me with his big thick body and his heavy-sounding footsteps. I followed him. He turned around when he heard me and looked annoyed. We were well into the woods then, and I lifted my skirt.

He didn't seem to notice, so I moved closer. He walked on. My feelings were hurt, but since I had already gone so far, I continued to follow him, moving close and touching him.... He slowed down. At first he spoke crossly to me in his usual way, but I walked on beside him, telling him how the sound of his footsteps in the hall made me sweat and how I was very lonely here. He finally stopped and held me, putting his big hands on my hips and straining me close where I could feel my effect on him. We went to the clearing. I undressed quickly and lay down for him, excited by his body if not by his actions. It was a disappointment. His thickness made him clumsy and he crushed my chest. He was so heavy I could not move and his movements were all the same, thump, thump, thump, with no teasing beginning or build up of intensity. Even his kiss was like that, squash, his mouth down on mine. But I still sweat when I hear him walking in the hall.

November 4th. Today something distressing happened. I found a whole section of five sheets torn out of a book, and the library has no other copy. I have written to the State Library for theirs. I must find out what a five-page scene would be like.

November 5th. I have been watching my friend's body. He is growing thicker. I wonder if it would work better with me on top. I try to convey this message to him by way of signs, such as stacking the linens outside my door on cleaning day with the thick pile of sheets on the bottom and the smaller pillowcases on top. He acts as if he doesn't notice, but I'm sure he must. He must notice me. I will go to his room the next time Mrs. Kesslar plays bridge.

November 13th. I went to his room as I said, but he pretended not to know what I wanted. He was very cross and his room was filled with the odor of cigar smoke and shoe polish. He seemed to have been blacking several pairs of boots that were standing in a row on the bed. No wonder his steps sound so heavy! I began to sweat immediately. I went to close the door, but he followed me and maneuvered it so that when the door closed I was outside. He called through the door that he had no equipment to make repairs of that kind, but I had seen a bottle of glue on his desk, and besides, he had surely known it wasn't the bedpost I was interested in. He is only playing hard to get.

November 16th. I am still waiting for the book from the State Library. It is a long time coming. Maybe it is loaned out. I hope whoever has it does not tear out the five pages.

November 21st. I lied again. There is no use lying in a journal. No one is impressed by the beauty of my confessions. No one is reading over my shoulder, though it sometimes seems as though I hear the foxy breathing of Mrs. Kesslar behind me when I am writing down some of the embarrassing things.

I didn't even go to the park that night. I stayed in my room and read some pages from my file and used the bedpost to get my satisfaction. I found a combination that works perfectly. A two-page scene of violence and seduction along with use of the bedpost. Only five minutes lost. That is all there is to sex anyway. Even when two people are involved, it is only a rubbing together of bodies. It is better alone. At least there is no pretense of closeness and none of the frustration of trying to be close and finding only walls. Here the walls are concrete; they separate me from everyone else. They are hideous, to be sure, with a lurid orange glow, but they can be touched, washed, painted, bumped against, struck. I know where they are.

November 25th. It is very cold here. The extra blanket is not enough. Mrs. Kesslar refuses to adjust the heat to the winter weather. She pretends to check the thermostat when I complain, but I can see that it is a dummy.

November 27th, Thanksgiving Day. There is, I think, no cause for thanks. Nothing has been given, nothing received, no donor, no recipient. No contact.

I am still the victim of my fancy stories. Four times I have told the wrong story of what happened in the park. This morning I resolved to write the truth exactly as it occurred, step by step. First my pen ran dry, and since it was a holiday, I could get no more ink. Mrs. Kesslar pretended to look in the pocket of her chair but did not find any ink to loan me. Then there was a fire in a house down the street. I went out and watched along with everyone else for blocks around.

A coal had fallen out of the fireplace while the family was eating dinner in the other room. People should not use fireplaces in this day of central heating. They only use them for illusion, not for warmth. They feel that by drawing near the fire they are not alone, that they also draw near to each other. They have many disappointments ahead, worse disappointments than the burning of their houses.

I came back to my room determined to write even if I had to use a pencil, but I am still unable to put down the truth. It is too embarrassing.

December 2nd. The book came from the State Library. The five pages were lies, every word a lie. I hate that sort of shabby fiction.

Why would anyone tear out such a sickening story? It was a seduction, all right, but with no violence. No bending of the will, no tearing. I am offended that such trash is allowed in the library. A mutual seduction! Totally unrealistic. I tore out the pages and burned them.

I must begin reading the books, reading them all, every book I can find, every page. Search out the lies and remove them. The world's libraries must not be filled with scenes like that, deceiving the innocent.

How can I hope to accomplish such a task? So many books, so many lies. So many lies to uncover and tear out.

Mrs. Kesslar stopped reading. One of the lodgers was paring his nails into an ashtray and didn't look up until the silence touched him.

"Is that all?" he asked.

At the change in voices, the other lodger nodded awake. He stretched, then reached for the remaining sugar wafer on the plate.

⋀⋄⋀⋁⋀⋁⋀

When the Gift Fits

In Highcastle, a town so old the structures rest on ruins three deep, yet so new the stereos and microwaves are powered from a nuclear power plant, the citizens walk the streets of ancient custom with the tread of modern concern. They make a modern living and raise a modern family, but occasionally one of them will trip over a bone or a shard left over from the past. So it happened to Aram Dodge, then an undistinguished young man of twenty-six.

Very early one February morning Aram was led to the still-dark living room of his small stone cottage by his dog Shaver, who was acting strangely. As he made his way, avoiding the familiar stacks of papers, his eyes picked out something on the coffee table that was less dark than the rest of the room. He waked up instantly at the alarming glow. Shaver bristled and growled. When Aram turned on a lamp to investigate, he found that he had become the Caretaker of the Gift.

Aram knew right away it was the Gift. That not-so-darkness made it unmistakable. In the same way a Scotsman boating on Loch Ness would know that an unexplained roiling from beneath meant Nessie, so a Highcastler knew that an unexplained phosphorescence on the coffee table meant the Gift.

His snap reaction was to be grateful. This could really help, he thought. Then all his feelings about the importance of his place in the world reorganized around his having become a person of note. He felt his torso wiggle as this new information changed him.

With a sense of participating in history he approached the coffee table. The container itself was about fifteen inches in diameter,

111

round and deep, with a double-curved divider in the middle marking off two sections shaped like yin and yang. It radiated faintly, but when Aram touched it, he found that it was cool and that it revolved in either direction on a base like a lazy Susan.

But the box was unimportant. What Aram was interested in right then was finding out what form the Gift had assumed for his tenure as Caretaker. He took a deep breath and opened it. Inside, lying one in the yin, the other in the yang, was a funny-looking pair of house slippers shaped like some his father used to wear before he died. His father had called them his "Faust slippers." Aram exhaled sharply.

He remembered his father's slippers with a twinge of old nausea, associating them with long bony feet and with being supervised on weekends by the owner of those feet. Made of green corduroy with the toe section separated from the heel by a curved V-shaped cut on either side, they had encased his father's impatient, nudging feet when Saturday morning cartoons had been switched off mid-chase in favor of chores. Aram had always dreaded the chores his father imposed on him to take the place of *Superman* and *Donald Duck*: shoveling snow, installing a septic system, spading a garden – always digging! – and the very tone of his father's preachy voice giving unneeded instructions could set him against whatever task it was.

These slippers, however, were made, not of green corduroy, but of soft white kid. After a moment's hesitation, he touched one. The kid felt powdery like an old woman's skin. Then, with the sense that there ought to be a witness to this absurdity, he tried it on. It fit perfectly. So did the other. A choking snort of laughter brought tears to his eyes and stung his nose. Here it was, the Gift, and all it turned out to be was a pair of slippers that were too daintsy-waintsy to be caught dead wearing. He put them back in the box.

His initial flush of hope faded into embarrassment. Being Caretaker of the Gift assured him a place in history if he chose to take it, but the place this Gift promised was not very dignified. He remembered one manifestation that occurred some years ago – an eighteen-room house. The Caretaker, a woman, had lived in it while she solved the puzzle of its meaning. Why couldn't he have been appointed Caretaker of something like that? But on the other hand, the

Gift had also been a pair of crutches once – and its last manifestation must have been a real doozy. That Caretaker had never made him or herself known. Perhaps a pair of slippers wasn't the worst that could happen.

Sipping his coffee in the kitchen, he couldn't help laughing again. Shaver reacted by wagging and prancing, clicking his toenails on the linoleum. Aram mechanically opened the door and let him out, still absorbed with the Gift and perplexed by who could have put it on his coffee table during the night. He had roused once when Shaver growled, but he hadn't really wakened up. Shaver growled at his own dreams and could be trusted only when he came right out and barked.

Someone, then, apparently known by the dog, had let him or herself in with a key and had cleared a spot on the table – pushing the pile of bills to one side – and damned if they hadn't emptied the ashtray and taken the dirty glasses to the kitchen! Aram stared at the row of glasses on his drain board. This down-to-earth touch was almost as amazing as the Gift itself.

He would have to take the day off. The receiver of the Gift shouldn't have to go to work. He wanted to tell Eleanor. This was too rich to savor alone. But he didn't want to tell her over the phone, so he waited until lunch time to meet her on the main street of Highcastle near her office – an unusual treat, because when he was at work, he went to lunch an hour later than she did.

Eleanor came swinging out the door of her building in her high-heeled boots and form-hugging coat with her long brown hair flying up as she met the February wind head on. He swung in step beside her. "Going my way?"

A quick glow of delight came over her face but changed immediately. Two little lines of worry appeared between her eyebrows. "What's the matter?"

"Nothing's the matter. I've got some news, that's all. Real news." Boy, would she be surprised!

She shook her hair out of her face. "Good or bad?"

"I'll tell you when we get to the restaurant. Let's go to The Place to Choose."

She stopped. "I don't have that kind of money."

"I'll use plastic. Come on." He steered her across the street to where the walkway got steep up the hill toward the castle.

After climbing a few steps she stopped again. "The answer is still no. If you're just trying to butter me up, forget it."

"Look, I'm telling you I've got news. Do you want to hear it or not?"

She gave him a searching look before taking his arm again. Her long hair blew against him as they climbed.

They had not been on the best of terms lately. There was the fight about living together and whether it should be at his place or hers, if at all. And under that fight was the one about getting married and having a child. Eleanor hadn't been spending the night recently. She was "giving serious thought," she had said.

At The Place to Choose they draped their coats over the extra chairs at a corner table. Aram, eager as he was to tell her the news, waited until they had gone to the cold buffet and loaded their plates.

"You should have been at my place this morning."

Instantly she slammed her fork down. "I knew it! I knew you were just trying to get me here so you could start pressuring me again. Well, don't bother. I am not going to move in with you. I am not going to spend the night there again, either, until I've had a chance to think things over. And if you don't stop pressuring me, I'm going to quit seeing you at all." She stared at him without moving while in the restaurant around them people laughed and clinked glasses and moved back and forth from the buffet tables.

If he hadn't wanted so badly to tell her about the Gift, Aram might have escalated the fight. He was tempted to say, "Who's pressuring whom?" and to point out the way she led him through the housewares department at Rolfes and talked about her sister's baby and how, if she herself ever had a baby, she wouldn't stick it in bed with a bottle. Talk about pressure. But he felt that a Gift Caretaker ought to be mature enough not to brawl with his girlfriend. He let their silence amid noise continue for a moment. "It was just a figure of speech," he said. "I was just going to tell you what happened."

He would have to be especially nice to her. Things had been

strained enough since his ex-roommate Steve's wedding at Christmas and had gotten really bad last month when she was late for her period. It had turned out okay, her period had started, but he knew she wanted to have a child, and it was out of the question for him. The very thought of getting himself tied down with a family turned him to jelly. Eleanor would just have to accept the fact that he wasn't ready to take on a responsibility like that.

"Well, what happened?" She speared a shrimp and dipped it into the puddle of red sauce on her plate.

"I've got the Gift."

Her face went blank. She shook her head, then brightened. "Well, it's about time. The wedding was two months ago."

"I'm not talking about a wedding gift," he said. "I'm talking about the Gift-gift. The biggie. The real thing. I've got it. It was on my coffee table when I woke up this morning."

She batted the palm of her hand against her ear. "Run that past me again."

He swallowed his bite of herring. "When I woke up this morning, Shaver was acting funny. You know, clicking his toenails like he wanted to go out, only when I got up, he wanted to go in the living room instead. And there on the coffee table was the Gift big as you please." He stopped to let it soak in.

Her look was more than skeptical. "How'd you know it was the Gift?"

"I just knew. You can tell those things. For one thing it glowed in the dark. You should have seen Shaver bristling up like it was some kind of offensive animal."

"My God, Aram, it's probably radioactive and you'll be sterile!"

He choked, coughed, and caught a piece of herring in his napkin. "That wouldn't be the worst thing in the world," he said. "But seriously, I don't think it's radioactive. I think it's a spiritual glow. Kind of like a halo, you know?"

"You're shitting me. You made up the whole thing as an excuse to take the day off. When you get home, it'll be gone without a trace."

"If you think I'm such a turd, how come you stick with me?"

"I don't know any who aren't turds." Then mischief flickered across her mobile face. "Besides, you aren't really solid enough to be a turd. You're more like a case of the runs."

He pushed his chair back. "On that disgusting note I'm going – going to proceed to the hot table. Join me?"

With fresh plates filled with hot delicacies before them, Eleanor settled into her chair with a more serious attitude.

"Okay, tell me the rest of the story. I don't even know what the Gift is. All I know is that it's got a halo." She was wearing her suspension-of-disbelief look.

"You're going to laugh. You won't be able to help it. Even I can't help it. It cracks me up." And he started laughing.

"Aram, if you really have the Gift, it's a very serious matter. Now stop laughing and tell me what it is."

"It's a pair of Faust slippers." He made a shushing gesture. "I know. You've never heard of Faust slippers. Okay. What they are is this. They're a kind of house slippers with the toe section and the heel section separate. Not joined by anything but the sole. My father used to have a pair." He frowned. "Green corduroy."

Eleanor was quiet. She took little sips of water that didn't lower the level in the glass. "How did they get there?"

"I haven't a clue. The legend says each Caretaker passes the Gift along to someone else, but I don't see how anyone could have gotten into my house. The only people who have a key are you and Mother."

"Could it have been your mother?"

"No way. I'd have known it if she'd been Caretaker of the Gift. If she calls me up to ask what she ought to have for dinner, she wouldn't keep a secret like that."

"How about Steve? Does he still have a key?"

"He may still have a key, but it couldn't have been him. Whoever left the Gift cleaned off the coffee table. If it had been Steve, he'd have added to the mess, not cleaned it up."

"Are you sure the door was locked?"

"Positive." Actually, he was not completely positive, but it had been locked this morning. He was almost positive.

"What I can't figure is why you. Isn't the Gift some kind of sacred trust?"

"Why not me? A person doesn't have to be a saint."

Eleanor looked at him curiously as though watching a snake shed its skin. "Look, I've got to get back to work. Are you going in this afternoon?"

"I hadn't planned on it."

She shrugged and stood up.

His plate was still half full, but he stood up too.

"You don't have to leave. If you're not going to work, you might as well stay here and finish your lunch."

"I've had all I want." Outside he said, "I know you're mad because I'm not at work, but it's not every day a person has something like this happen. It's like a birthday. A person shouldn't have to go to work on a day like this."

"Whatever." She started running and ran all the way down the hill, jaywalking through red lights and cutting around pedestrians. How she could run on cobblestones in those high heels amazed him. When she reached the street her office was on, she waited for him and said, "This isn't going to change a thing, is it?"

"What should it change?" he asked. "Of course it's going to change things. It's supposed to change things!" He had to hurry to keep up with her. "I don't know what you're talking about."

"I haven't time to explain it now. I care about my job even if you don't care about yours."

"Just one thing." He caught her arm. "It wasn't by any chance you, was it?"

"Me who had the Gift and gave it to you?" She went inside. "Don't be ridiculous."

Aram stood there for a moment. Her reaction certainly wasn't all it could have been. She didn't have to be so moody. But the Gift was still on his mind, and his new status as Caretaker, and he thought he ought at least to try and see things from her point of view. The pregnancy scare had to have been worse for her than it was for him. That was undoubtedly still weighing on her.

For Ellie's sake he considered going in to work and telling them he was feeling better, but he decided not to. He owed the rest of the day to himself. He worked as a paralegal – a gofer – at a law office.

Let the attorneys walk to the courthouse, he thought. Let them make their own coffee. This was one day he wasn't going to spend gofering. Ellie was already mad and he couldn't change that, so he might as well enjoy himself.

Back home he did some more cleaning. No wonder whoever left the Gift had tidied up, he thought. The place wasn't fit to house something that special. It wasn't really disgusting, the way it had been when Steve shared the house with him, but it hadn't been cleaned since Christmas, either. Bare stalks of poinsettias with nothing left but a splash of red on top sat in their foil-covered pots. His bicycle lay in sections on the floor; he had planned to get it in riding condition by spring. Also, there were a few dishes and pans on the floor beside the chair where he watched TV – no garbage, thanks to Shaver, but some plates and a skillet. It didn't look good.

As he worked, his thoughts turned to how he might make use of the Gift. It would be okay to use it, wouldn't it? He wasn't sure. The legend didn't point out the moral obligations of the Caretaker. Only that the Caretaker was supposed to discover the Gift's meaning and then pass it on to someone else. But in the Bible story about the talents, the servants who had used theirs had been rewarded, while the one who had hidden his away had been punished. If he used the Gift, maybe he would be rewarded in some way. But even as he considered it, he felt like laughing again. The only way to use a pair of slippers was to wear them, and there was no way he would wear anything that looked like that.

In the evening he phoned Ellie. Maybe he could get her to come over and see the Gift for herself. She might change her attitude. There was no answer, not even for voice mail. He drank a six-pack and watched TV and slept on the couch.

Aram took the next day off, too, and the next. In fact, he never went back to the law office again. Each morning he would wake up with the Gift on his mind, and he knew it was out of keeping for a Caretaker to file briefs and carry coffee for attorneys who had done nothing to deserve such service except stick it out in law school longer than he had.

Eleanor called him "leisure class" in a sarcastic tone, but she didn't break off with him.

His mother clipped "Help Wanted" ads, which he ignored.

His own regret about quitting work was that he hadn't had time yet to use the firm's backing to have his name legally changed. He hated the name "Aram," another of his dead father's bequests. He hated it because it sounded ethnic and he was not ethnic. It also rhymed with "harem" as he remembered very well from his playground days. But he could probably get the name change even without an attorney. He had already done the research, had copied the cites, and he could file the brief for himself. So he stayed at home "leisure class" and looked to the Gift for inspiration.

The Gift wasn't very helpful along this line. It just sat there on the coffee table with the unpaid bills and offered no inspiration at all. Aram was left to his own devices, and he did the same things ordinary people do when they don't have to go to work. He watched TV and listened to music and as spring came along, he sometimes went outdoors and threw a stick for Shaver to fetch. It got pretty boring after a while. But this was a small price to pay for the honor of being Caretaker of the Gift.

Sometimes he would take the Faust slippers out of their box and put them on. He got used to the way they looked and after a while he even began to admire them, though he still wouldn't let anyone see him wearing them. He would just put them on and stick his feet up on the hassock and admire the elegant way they looked. But before long, they would start to hurt. No one spot, no particular pressure point, no slipping heel or pinching toe. They fit perfectly. He couldn't put his finger on the problem, but after a while wearing them, his feet would be killing him. He would have to take them off and put them back in the box.

This rankled. Another thing rankled too: the way people treated him about being Caretaker. He had thrown a party to celebrate, and his friends treated it as a joke. He should have known. They understood the Gift, all right, but they couldn't seem to get it through their heads how important it was that he was the Caretaker. They were more interested in what he served to eat and drink and smoke than they were in his possibilities as Caretaker. They didn't take the name change seriously either. He had gone ahead and changed it to Adam – oh, the significance of a single letter! – but none of them ever called him that. He thought about writing his friends off and making others, but nothing came of it. They kept on being his friends anyway and ignoring the things that were important.

Adam still pondered endlessly where the Gift had come from, who had had it before and what it might have been. One Sunday when he was having a chicken dinner at his mother's, he asked her point blank if she had given it to him.

She answered him point blank, "No." If she had ever possessed such a thing, she said, she wouldn't have given it to her only son to be the ruination of him.

He was taken aback. His mother had never spoken to him that way before. So that was what she thought of him! He couldn't bring himself to face her anymore and started making excuses to avoid going to see her.

If his mother thought this ill of him, it was a good thing his father was no longer alive. He'd have thought even worse. His father had been a stickler for the ordinary; he had no flair whatsoever for the special. He approved of things like staying in school, getting a better job, bringing home a paycheck, bettering yourself – the yoke over the shoulders. Adam had had a dream about his father recently; it had been just as it was in his childhood, his father coming up the back walk from the alley after work. He wore his dirty work clothes and his boots. He slammed the kitchen door behind him and handed Mom his paycheck and asked her what's for dinner just like always, and then he stooped over the kitchen sink and washed just the way he always did. He never called it "washing his face;" he called it "washing his neck and ears." Mom was the one who called it "washing her face." But the funny thing was that whatever they called it, they both washed it all: face, and neck, and ears. When his finished washing in the dream, he put on his slippers and gave Adam a little nudge in the backside. "Got your homework done?" he asked, and Adam was just as furious in the dream as Aram had been in reality.

His mother's calling it "ruination" was uncomfortably close to the truth. He knew it. Here he was, many weeks into Caretaking without having benefited in any way. He was out of money. Since he no longer went to see his mother, he couldn't very well borrow any more from her. If he was supposed to Caretake, he ought to be free to do so, he thought. This meant that the Gift out to support him so that he could Caretake well.

But how? He chewed over the puzzle for a long time while he went through most of his friends, borrowing more and more money. He even approached Eleanor, but she wouldn't give him any. In a way, he was relieved.

Finally the answer came. He would go into business. Offer the public an opportunity to view the Gift for a fee, like the people on the hill showed the Castle. He arranged plush-covered ropes outside his house so that nobody could push ahead in line, and he chained Shaver out back. He put up a sign. "View the Gift," it said. "Saturdays and Sundays nine to five. Senior citizens half price. Babes in arms free." It didn't behoove a Caretaker to be overly greedy.

The venture was a success. The Gift, of course, had the legend behind it and the fame of its past Caretakers, at least the ones who hadn't kept their status a secret. The media covered Adam's opening, interviewed him and put his story out to the public, which then flocked to stand within the velvet ropes waiting for a glimpse of the Gift, which glowed obligingly on the coffee table.

After a while even foreigners came, scholars from the Library of Congress and the British Museum doing folklore studies. Tourists came from Japan, making Adam's place a side trip from their tours of Yellowstone and the Taj Mahal and the Eiffel Tower. English schoolteachers came and German walkers. Solemn Nigerians, their black faces shining over their summer suits. Every weekend morning there would be people standing outside before nine o'clock waiting for him to chain the barking Shaver out back and open for business.

Eleanor more or less came around to his way of thinking. She still wouldn't live with him, but she guided the tour while he sat at the door and took the money. Eleanor had a nice musical voice, and she told the story of the Gift well:

"The Gift you are viewing today is the modern version of a tradition shrouded in the mists of antiquity. No one knows when or where it started, but it has been a part of our culture at least as long as the Grail legends – and the Gift is a lot more democratic than the Grail.

Anyone can be a Caretaker; you don't have to go on a quest or be pure or ask the right questions." And Eleanor would tell some anecdotes from the sourcebooks about individuals in history who had been Caretakers and about the mystery of the Gift's changing form. People would ask why the modern version was a pair of Faust slippers. She would answer that no one knew. Adam would find out eventually, she said, and when he did, it would be time for him to pass the Gift to someone else for whom it would take a different form.

Adam, of course, asked no questions about the Gift's form. He made no attempt to find out anything that would even hint that he ought to pass it on. He was not the least bit ready to go back to gofering. He sat at the door and took the money and listened to Eleanor give the speech. He would have gone on like this forever. Boring as it was, it was better than working.

He was richer, too. He now owned a Porsche instead of a Schwinn, and designer clothes. He looked forward to a comfortable future and decided it was time to talk marriage to Ellie. After planning and rehearsing the event in his mind, he took her to a jewelry store and formally proposed.

To his surprise she turned him down. "I need more security than this. I want to have children and be able to quit my job and take care of them. At least for a while."

"You can quit your job right now if you want to. We're rolling in money."

"This Gift thing can't last forever. You know that as well as I do."

"I've got money saved."

"That's not the same. It just doesn't make me feel secure like a good, steady, dependable job would."

Eleanor's assessment cooled his enthusiasm for the business. It was as though every time he thought about it, which was practically all the time, he had not only his own view of it but hers as well, like a double vision. It made for tension.

What he needed, he thought, was some relief, some other activity. To this end he started going drinking with his old buddy Steve on the nights when Eleanor did laundry and Steve's wife Tess bowled with her league.

He and Steve were at the tavern drinking one night when a drunk came from the other end of the bar. "Aren't you the guy with the Gift?" he asked in a trouble-seeking tone. Adam saw him in the bar mirror without turning around. He looked like trouble too.

Steve was the one who answered. "We sure are." Steve was big and bushy-haired and nobody messed with him.

"I'm talkin' to your friend here." The tone was more conciliatory. "I just wanna ask him how come he don't wear them slippers, get some use out of them instead of leaving them set in the box all day. What good's a Gift you never use?"

"He does," Steve answered. "I didn't when I had it, but he does. Those slippers may be on display in the box on weekends, but he uses them all the time during the week."

Adam stared at Steve. Steve grinned and biffed his shoulder. The drunk went back to his seat at the other end of the bar.

"Didn't you guess it was me?"

"I didn't think you could have kept it a secret right under my nose."

"I forgot I even had it," said Steve. "It was stuck back in the glove box of my car."

Adam pictured the round container in Steve's glove box. No way. Then he remembered. "What was it?"

"Well, it was something really useless, you know, and as soon as I noticed how useless it was, I knew it was useless because I wasn't using it, and at that point it was time to pass it on."

Adam was too drunk to follow the logic. "But what was it?" It had to be something even worse than Faust slippers or Steve would have told him.

"It was a little bitty ring. I couldn't even get it past the tip of my finger. So I stuck it away. I didn't even think about it until Tess found it and tried it on. I couldn't very well give it to her, because it would have changed into something else, so I bought her one, and the rest is history."

"Hell, man, you could have done a lot with that," said Adam enviously. "You missed a good thing. Look what it's done for me." He swaggered a little in his Pierre Cardin jacket. "A ring would have been even better. You wouldn't have had to put up with the element that thinks a pair of Faust slippers is comical."

"What I want to know is this," said Steve, ignoring the jacket. "What I want to know is how come you never wear the things?"

"Because they hurt," exclaimed Adam. "There's something funny about them. When I first put them on, they feel fine, but after a little while, I feel like a damn cripple." He finished his drink and made a sign to the bartender for another. "You told that guy that I use them, but I don't. They hurt too bad."

"Ah," said Steve, "but you do use them. You *use* them every day, Monday through Friday. You just don't *wear* them."

This didn't make sense. Tourists came on Saturday and Sunday. Even if allowing the public to view them could be called *using* them. "You're fulla shit," said Adam.

Steve biffed him on the shoulder again, harder this time. "Listen," he said, "You use them every Monday through Friday to keep from going to work."

This was too much, even for a best friend. But Adam wasn't big enough to take on Steve, and besides, what could he say?

That night before he went to bed Adam put on the Faust slippers. He didn't have them on five minutes before his feet began to feel like they were dissolving. He kicked them off hastily. "Why *Faust* slippers?" he wondered, for the first time.

His dream that night was about the slippers, of course. He had them on and was determined to wear them no matter how much they hurt. His feet felt like they were melting away. Soon he would have nothing below his knees but little pointed sticks. But he kept on wearing them. Then the dream changed. Now a tourist had picked them up and was examining the soles. The tourist took out a knife and hacked the slippers apart, laid the white kid pieces over Adam's feet, and put the soles in his pockets. The dream changed again. Now the slippers didn't hurt any longer and Adam had his feet back, but neither were they white kid any longer. They were his own old house slippers, a pair of fleece-lined moccasins Eleanor had given him, a pair of ordinary slippers like thousands of others.

Late in the night Adam awakened from the dream and got up. It was all over. He knew it. He went in the living room. The box on the coffee table didn't glow any longer. He groped around on the floor to find where he had kicked the slippers. Only one of them was there. It took him half an hour to find what was left of the other one under his bed chewed to a pulp. Shaver did not respond to his stern call. Adam found him in the basement behind the furnace.

It was time for him to pass the Gift along, and tired as he was, he could not ignore the imperative. He dressed and took the box with the one good slipper and the pulpy mess across town to a house he had never seen before, the house of a stranger. The stranger had not been careful enough to lock his door, so Adam went inside easily. He shone his flashlight around, wondering where to place the Gift. This stranger had no coffee table. Already the Gift was changing shape, right in Adam's hands. The urge to hurry was strong, so Adam simply put down the now unrecognizable package on the stranger's TV. He locked the door as he left.

On the way home he had a moment of panic when he realized that he should have given it to Eleanor, kept in the family where it could keep on doing some good. But that wasn't such a hot idea. Having the Gift would change Ellie, and he wasn't sure how that might turn out.

When the sun rose, he went out and took down the signs. He coiled up the velvet ropes and put them in his basement. He sat for a long time looking at the scrapbook about himself as Caretaker, then put the scrapbook away. It was like an album of vacation pictures, good to look through, but the vacation was over.

Adam went back to the law office that morning and found that someone else was the gofer now. He would not be rehired, not after the irresponsibility he had shown. And the more he thought about it, the less he wanted to be a gofer all his life. He would have to go back to law school, he thought, morosely. He wasn't a Caretaker any longer. He was just one more of the unemployed. But at least he had some money saved. And it wouldn't take forever to finish law school if he busted ass.

He walked down the main street of Highcastle toward where Eleanor still worked, careful not to walk too slowly, like an unemployed person. As he neared her building he stumbled over something, and when he looked down, he saw that it was a well-chewed rawhide dog bone lying on the sidewalk. Catching his balance, he biffed one hand into the palm of the other. "Why a ring?" he wondered. He would ask Steve to spell it out. But he was going to have to pass the bar exam and get some clients before he brought it up. Only then would he be able to hold his head up and admit why Faust slippers.

.Λ.Λ.Λ.Λ.

Amelioration

Tomorrow morning before anyone is up I am going to abandon my consuming household with its incessant needs and move myself alone into a mini-warehouse. There, surrounded by voiceless concrete walls, my only view of the outside world a star going by the ventilation hole at night, I am going to start over, think one single thought all the way to its conclusion, and on this conclusion base the rest of my life. I shall take measured steps in a well-mapped direction toward a known goal. No more unconscious groping. No more yearning. No more pregnancies that result in a geometric confusion of my purpose. For $37.50 a month I am going to put myself in storage in a place that would otherwise be wasted on surplus lawn furniture and back issues of dying magazines. I am going to figure out what went wrong and how to make it right.

But it is getting late and I must make preparations. I must pack the rest of my belongings and leave instructions for everyone and write a letter to Harris even though it's only Tuesday. I must write notes, make lists:

To Houseclean:

The Christmas wrappings have mildewed in the dampness on the basement floor; you must do something. Christmas is necessary.

Get Sears to fix the dryer or hang the laundry on the line outside – if you can get Digger to tighten it; otherwise, there's a clothes prop out by the fence, or if you'd rather, you can use the Laundromat or string lines in the basement. You'll find a way.

At seven o'clock each evening you are to collect everything the children have not put away and give it promptly to the Goodwill. Everything. You must be heartless about it. I've been meaning to try this technique for a long time; it is said to produce habits of tidiness in children in a matter of days.

Mop the kitchen when Cook asks you and sweep up the mud Digger tracks in and keep Harris's mother's commode emptied so that there will be no more disasters with the ceiling plaster and be kind to the children and remember that you are answerable.

To Digger:

Hoe the corn, water the tomatoes, spray the squash, hill up the leeks, dust the cabbage – but don't disturb the balance of nature.

Bring in whatever Cook wants for dinner and teach the children to care for growing things and tend the flowers as though they were as important as the vegetables, and remember that you are answerable.

To Cook:

Save the beans, wrap the cheese, keep the lid on the garbage and set the table before the guests arrive. Do not pay more than $1.89 for butter.

Put the bones from everyone's plate into the stock pot but don't let them see you do it.

Find the recipe we discussed and use up the split pig's foot before it gets freezer burn. The recipe was in a cookbook we had from the library. I don't remember the dish but the split pig's foot was mentioned as a possible addition, for its gelatinous quality. You'll find it, I'm sure. One mustn't waste good food.

Consult with Nurse about nutrition and with Digger about menu planning. See that there is no junk food in the house.

Permit the children to help with the cooking and feed Houseclean a bland diet for her ulcer and restrict Harris's mother's water consumption, and remember that you are answerable.

To Nurse:

Tell Digger to get rid of the poison ivy right away and in the meantime wash the boys with detergent.

Clean up the little ones before dinner; one must set standards. Do not allow ANY dogs to eat out of the children's plates.

When the high school calls back about classes for the Special Child, tell them we've got one, and when the police call back about the stolen bicycle, tell them there is good reason to believe it has been painted green.

Remember the children's birthdays and buy them gifts. The list is in the blue book on the desk. Check it each month except April so that no child will be forgotten.

Take Harris's mother out for a drive on Sundays and unplug the upstairs phone so that she won't keep getting obscene phone calls and tell her again and again that we've already planted a snowball bush on Henry's grave and change her sign with the day and date every morning, and don't forget that you are answerable.

To my children:

Help with the housework, the gardening, the cooking and the care of each other; look after the animals because if you don't, they will go to the pound and be caged and then killed, though humanely.

Write to your father each week and tell him your grades and achievements so that he will know he is a good father.

Brush your teeth and your hair and never talk to strangers; I have given you life, but it is up to you to maintain it, and remember that once born, you are answerable.

To my friend and neighbor Sonja:

Please do not worry about me and if you are my true friend, do not spread it around that I have gone crazy.

I have tried your solutions and found that they did not work out for me: the twenty pounds came back, the fur coat got moths, and the lover moved to Chicago and left me his boxer puppy to housebreak. This time I'll try a new solution.

I know you're going to wonder who will support me now that my ass is all stretched out and nobody will buy it. I wish you to know that I have a weekly tryst set up with the ATM, who cares nothing about cellulite. He likes to have me cycle his buttons while he sucks my credit card. When he comes, he comes new twenty dollar bills.

And this brings me to the favor I want to ask of you. If the police or the fire engines show up at my house, please leave word with the ATM and he will relay the message. I don't want anyone to know where I am, and I don't want to be bothered with minor emergencies – diaper rash, expulsions from school. Use your best judgment, Sonja, and consider me still your friend, Amelia.

With the notes and lists all written except the letter to Harris, I am almost ready to go, but I'm afraid. I know myself. I'm an Amelia with no backbone. When the walls of the mini-warehouse press down on me, I'll come creeping back and stand at the fence looking in the windows. I'll write lists and put them in the milk box where Cook can't fail to find them; I'll remind them to wash the combs in ammonia water and tell them to get the dogs their rabies shots and I'll clip that ad for a dry wreath that might go well on Henry's grave.

If only I'd been named Audrey instead of Amelia I'd have been different. An Audrey wouldn't take upon herself the task of amelioration, smoothing angry waters, accommodating to distractions, preserving amenities. The very name Audrey augers an augmented life, an audacity, a moving out from home and blowing up trouble now and then. I think it says something that they've never named a hurricane "Amelia."

Or maybe I'd have done better as an Athene developing the life of the mind. If I'd been an Athene from the start, I'd not have married Harris and become the administrator of this estate. I'd have gone to live with a wise man in sandals, the kind with a loop for the big toe. He'd have had a house on the alley with no address, a single-room house built of fieldstone with a fireplace in the center. We'd have sat by the fire, first on one side, then another, and I'd have grown wiser instead of bigger in front. Isn't that what an Athene would have wanted? We'd have spoken carefully about one thing and another in order, with pauses in between for thinking. My life would have unfolded like the slow unrolling of a scroll and the pain of growth would have been a series of small pin-pricks, not this anguish of amputation that is now required, with hair-raising dreams of pain in the missing limb, of children gone wrong, of the house burning down.

But fear or no fear I have already rented the mini – #441, 934 Progress Village, which is as sterile an expanse of concrete as one could imagine, lying between the freeway and the gas works. I have placed inside it a light bulb, a camp stove, a cot and a gray granite slop jar. Two buckets stand in the corner, one for carrying clean water in, the other for carrying dirty water out. I hung a flowered curtain on one wall to serve as an imaginary window so that I could pretend I had only to pull back the curtain and look out if I wanted. All that is left to move is myself; that will take place before dawn and then I shall sit on the cot and wait.

And now the letter to Harris:

June 15th

My dear husband:

I am going for a trip of uncertain length and won't be here in case your expedition should end or you should try to phone me.

Everything here has been going much as usual, the children are getting taller and so are the weeds. Our friends are splitting up in middle age – with much acrimony – it's a pity they couldn't have seen the wisdom of our way, leaving spaces in our togetherness right after the ceremony so as to save the marriage. The sermon last Sunday was entitled "Brighten the Corner" and it made me feel weary.

I hope you are in good health and that your objective is set well in front of you instead of off to one side or worse, left behind.

Be sure to record your thoughts and take your vitamin C and pray for our salvation.

I have had a new roof put on and the bare spot covered with sod and I take your mother to the doctor and the hairdresser and the cemetery, and I have one question to ask you: Do you ever think of me and if so, what do you think? Is there anything you could think that would correspond to me myself?

God bless you,
your loving wife, Amelia

P.S. You'd better send the next sperm by regular post. The parcel service let the last batch thaw. But I won't be here anyway, so it probably doesn't matter.

/V\·V\·V\·V\

October 15th

Dear Sonja:

Because there has been no message from you these past four months I assume nothing has gone wrong at my house, though I know better, of course. Something goes wrong at my house every day. I am removed, however; I do not even go back to look in the windows.

I am writing to give you a change of address. The ATM has been a disappointment. I am going to discontinue the relationship. There are times when I forget my PIN number. I cycle and cycle and he sucks and sucks, but nothing further happens. If I can't be more than a number to him, I will have nothing to do with his dreary problems.

You can contact me through Post Office Box 24, Alamo Station. Why I didn't think of this at the outset I don't know. It's so clean, having only a business connection with your address.

I have another success to report. When I realized that I was pregnant again, I felt most embarrassed, thinking I would have to ask still another favor of you, for after all, I have given up the responsibility of caring for other people. I had thought: I'll ask Sonja to be on the lookout, to keep her eyes open for a doorstep that cries out for a baby! It was to be a doorstep lined with flowers, with a squash vine, perhaps, and the window was to be sparkling clean for the baby to look out. That is how silly I was, not realizing that in the months ahead the window will be shuttered against the cold, the squash vine will be covered with snow, and if there are any flowers by the doorstep, they will be plastic and I would not offer a baby to a doorstep lined with plastic flowers. But I then thought of the solution myself, a success! I know just such a doorstep: I used to live behind it. In April I will present Nurse with the gift of another child which I know she will appreciate, since without a steady supply of babies to care for, her work would come to an end.

May the winter sunlamp preserve your summer tan, may your roots never grow out gray, and may your cream-colored carpet never curdle. With these and other best wishes I remain,

Your friend,
Amelia

/\/\/\/\/\/

A proper tone of optimism, I think. Only the high points, not the jagged paths leading up to them. And certainly no mention of the quite reasonable assumption that if I am prone to forget my PIN number, I shall certainly forget my post office box number as well. One makes the gesture. I would not tell this story to anyone, let alone Sonja.

I have been living these four months in a space ten by ten, free from the stresses of arbitration and administration, but subject to all the indignities weather can inflict. The heat has been endurable, but barely; the cold is becoming unendurable so rapidly that I shall have to make a change very soon.

The body inflicts indignities too. The only good thing about the body is that it is thin for the first time in years, though it won't stay that way long. The reason it is thin is that I eat and drink as little as possible. I am faced with the body as a recycler of food and drink, a kind of compost maker in which dinner becomes manure overnight and a cup of tea is changed in minutes into high grade liquid fertilizer. These products must be disposed of, and in secret, because my landlord doesn't know he is my landlord and I use all cunning to keep him from finding out. We are animals, and nothing has ever demonstrated this to me so convincingly as the absence of plumbing. We recycle, and we reproduce.

I am not complaining. Being here has advantages. I am responsible for myself and myself alone. I do not hold the reins that guide Houseclean, Digger, Cook, Nurse, all those children I inflicted on myself, the waxing and waning of the dog pack, the flourishing and decay of plants. I have only my own pee to cope with, not that of the old and incontinent, or the young and incontinent, or the willfully incontinent.

It was through this coping that I discovered early on that I was not alone in this complex. My unexpected neighbor lived across and two doors down. He had been watching my comings and goings, he told me – and I was immediately disposed against him. One of the reasons I came here was to escape being continually in the gaze of someone else.

He said he had observed me until he felt sure his attention would be welcome, then came around hoping for companionship. I could tell what that meant. Another strike against him, along with his cobwebby jeans so thin as to reveal not only white pathetic knees but also curled black hair and an unkempt circumcision that refused to be stared down. As it looked at me with its one tearful eye, I remembered my decision to seek out companionship only when I wanted it and never to allow myself to be sought.

He told me my demeanor made him feel comfortable and secure. This sounded just like home, where everything rested on me and I rested on nothing. It was ridiculous: all he could have seen of me was a woman, furtive, in the moonlight, emptying a slop jar down the drain hole outside. I blush.

I told him I was hiding from the people and responsibilities that pursued me and that if I were found, I would have to go back and continue what I had been doing so satisfactorily to everyone but myself.

He confided that he was in trouble with the law and that if he were found, he would have to go back to be prevented from doing what was satisfying to himself but reprehensible to others. "We are not so different, are we?" he said. "It all comes down to being wanted."

With no encouragement whatsoever, he inflicted on me the nature of his crime. I'd thought drugs, probably. He was the right age. But no, he said, they wanted him on a trumped-up charge of child molesting. He was outraged, said he hadn't molested the child, that she'd enjoyed it as much as he had and what was so goddam sacred about a child, anyway? "Children are sexy little beasts," he said, "just like everyone else. Why deny them the pleasures of life?"

At this I swirled myself into a real Audrey of a mid-summer ice storm and emptied the contents of my gray granite slop jar over his head. My capacity for listening had shrunk to nothing within minutes. "Out!" I screamed. "Get out! Children should take their pleasures with each other, not with the likes of you!" And I pushed him, slimy as he was, to the edge of the complex. I'd have ridden him out on a rail if there'd been someone to carry the other end.

He started to slink away, then turned like a cur and snarled, "I know where your children are, bitch!"

"You don't even know who I am," I answered. But I went to the phone booth on the freeway and called the police just in case. I was glad my comings and goings had not included visits back home to peek in the windows.

So much for unwanted companionship.

I stayed in my ten by ten, going out only for food and water, and to empty my odorous slop jar. I slept a great deal and when I slept, I dreamed. Over and over again I dreamed of babies, of pregnancy, of giving birth, of suckling. When I awakened my body would be drawn up in some wrenched position and I would suffer the most acute discomfort. I endured this for weeks, thinking it would change, but it did not. Every time I slept there was a baby. Every time I wakened there was suffering.

And so I went out in search of relief, thinking exercise would help me. I walked in the early morning and the late evening. I walked the alleys so that I would see no one who knew me. After walking I would return to my cell and sleep all the more soundly with all the more vivid dreams of babies.

One afternoon I slept in the August heat. Flies buzzed around me, avoiding the flypaper curling down from the ceiling. I could hear

them nagging me even as my dreaming womb expanded; in the confusion of sleep their buzzing became buzzards waiting for me. When
I awakened, I realized the baby in the dream had been a little Amelia,
complete with tightly-curled hair and dimple in the left cheek. I felt
sick, as though tumbled through a wash-dry cycle. I sprayed my ten
by ten to kill the flies, then closed the door and left.

By then it was evening. I walked a long way through familiar alleys where shrub tangles had overrun the fences and spread out so
that only a footpath remained. Nightshade vines, rose brambles and
mulberry shoots had taken over. As I walked, a summer storm came
up, small puddles formed quickly in the path, new rain made silver
bubbles that burst in the dark gray pools. The wind cleaned and
cooled the air and broke the heat, which would have been a relief if
I hadn't been so wet and chilled and far from home. I walked briskly
in the right direction but when enough time had gone by to get me
there, I found myself in still another alley with still more rose brambles and puddles of water. It was there that I smelled wood smoke
and in another moment came upon a little house that stood smack
against the alley — the kind of place that must have once been a
garage. The door was open. I looked in and saw that the smoky odor
was coming from the chimney pipe of a stove in the middle.

Such a strange place! The walls were covered completely with
rolled-up scrolls, like the map of the world that Miss Cory used to
pull down over the spelling words in third grade.

I was wondering what kind of person could use so many such
maps when a man opened the screen door, inviting me to enter.

I did so. He gave me a towel and a cup of Cutty Sark for which I
was grateful. I dried myself and sat by the stove sipping the Cutty
Sark until I could stop shivering. Then I thanked him and said I
thought I should start out again for my little ten by ten with the flies
now waiting to be swept up off the floor. "Where am I?" I asked.
"What is the address here?" If I knew the address I could find my way
back.

"There is no address," he answered. "I get my mail from a post office box." He looked extremely pleased at this arrangement, his eye
wrinkles digging into his face, the scalp wrinkles on his shining head

awry like furrows plowed by a farmer high in his air-conditioned trac-
tor cab reading *Mad Magazine* up and down the rows.

"What about the phone book? Isn't there some kind of address in
the phone book?"

"I have no phone." He looked even more pleased, his eroded
head and upper face giving way to the soft lush down of a tidily
mowed beard.

Two fleeting thoughts: one, that even we hermits have a community; the other, that the post office box was a good idea, the ATM already having shown symptoms of his difficulties. Then the Cutty
Sark finished its take over of my sparsely fed and watered body.

"You'll stay," said the man. He by now resembled a contour globe
with crags and veldts, his massive chest endless like the steppes of
central Asia.

I nodded, looking down. On the floor I saw his feet and suddenly
knew where I was and why. The feet were housed in homemade sandals, the soles of which were tire treads, the loops cut strips of a wash
cloth I recognized as part of a set popular five years ago at the Green
Stamp store. Here was the wise man in sandals, I thought, and I was
brought here to ask my question.

I blurted it out, I think, while he was still explaining why it would
be better for me to go home in the morning since it was now quite
dark and I would never find my way.

Then he arranged his poor pallet near the stove, spread it with a
fur rug, and we lay there together for the night.

When I awakened the next morning, he had gone and I was pregnant. I found the Alka-Seltzer and the coffee and I helped myself to
his gracious indoor plumbing.

Then I looked around. The maps of the walls intrigued me, so
neatly rolled, so like my third grade classroom. I thought fondly of
Miss Cory and how I had been, for that one lovely year, teacher's pet.
I would look, now, at the maps of the wise man and perhaps my question would be answered.

I pulled down the one by the door. It was not a map. Instead of
some intricate portrayal of the backbone of South America, there on
the wise man's wall, pulled down as though over the spelling words,

was an enlarged version of the *Playboy* centerfold for February 1974.
I snapped it back up and tried another. September 1969. April 1971.
I tried them all, round the walls, faster and faster, carelessly ripping
a tit on Miss June '76 as I hastened to view Miss December '77.

On the last scroll, instead of a picture, was a list of women's names,
hundreds of them, and at the end was my name, Amelia, with a tidy
little note beside it, "Remember that you are answerable."

The Almost Perfect Flaw

Every man finds himself unaccountably attracted to certain imperfections in women. Indeed, women with bony feet, fat bottoms or thin hair, and every grotesquery in between, do find partners, proving that no flaw exists without admirers. Usually the defect is slight: a mole, a malocclusion – perhaps even a strange pigmentation – -but occasionally it is so exaggerated as to be the woman's only noteworthy characteristic. Where the magnetism originates, no one knows.

Billy Malkin, too, had his taste in women, though his circumspect life at the bank did not permit him to indulge it satisfactorily. Hardly a day passed without the other tellers, older women, all of them, teasing him about settling down with some nice young lady, cackling at him when the pretty girls ignored the shorter lines at their windows so as to get their paychecks cashed by a young man with possibilities. They needn't have pushed it, because it was the respectable thing to do, and Billy wanted badly to be respectable. But he was powerless. The Friday girls gathering their energy for the weekend terrified him. They were not at all to his taste.

The woman Billy dreamed of was a perfect doll of a girl who never spoke, small and thus appealing, for Billy always felt himself shrivel in the presence of large, lively girls with their loud laughter and pushy ways. His girl would be frail and light enough to carry in his arms with her long, dark hair swinging down over his elbow – and she would have been stricken in youth by a death that did not leave marks.

Only once in his thirty-four years had he known such a girl, a perfect one. Her name was Ida.

She had been in his Latin classes all through high school, her classic profile swathed in long, black hair as she recited her way from "*Omnia Gallia in tres partes divisa est,*" through "*Delenda est Carthago,*" into "*Credula res amor est,*" in her quiet voice that had echoed through his dreams for all these years.

Every day in Latin class Billy had watched her, wishing for her to notice him but afraid she might.

Ida had grown paler and thinner and Billy had become more and more enamored, and then one day she hadn't come to class. Rumors about the seriousness of her illness went around. At last the announcement came: she had died.

That evening Billy checked the obituaries and went to pay his respects. He signed the book, surprised to find himself the only one from school to fulfill his obligation to the dead. He spoke well of her to her mother, mentioned her studiousness and pronunciation, then felt a surge of excitement as he approached the casket.

Her mother led him by the sleeve, talking gratefully, not noticing his response. She left him at the casket with his head bowed. He thought he'd better pray and did: "Hail Caesar! We who are about to die salute you!" with the odor of carnations strong like a wilted corsage and his hands in his pockets trying to hide his erection.

The bowed head was interpreted as grief — as it was, truly. Ida's mother sounded Billy out. "You young people must have been seeing quite a lot of each other."

"Almost every day," Billy answered, not mentioning that it was only in Latin class.

"I work two jobs and haven't been able to spend the time with Ida that I wanted to. I'm sure she was very fond of you."

"Yes'm," he answered, emboldened. Surely he could respond to the woman's pleading for her daughter's happiness, albeit too late. "We were very fond of each other."

"It helps to know that." The woman's voice trembled, and Billy found himself comforting her with a tentative pat.

This conversation seemed no more bizarre to Billy than the funeral parlor itself. He had never been in such a place before, never seen a dead person or talked to a grieving mother.

Thus when Ida's mother invited him to sit with the body the next evening so that she could get some rest, he agreed, feeling more than honored.

His vigil was memorable. Few viewers called. As the evening grew late and he was sure that he was alone, Billy paced in front of the casket, taking away some of the flowers and viewing the body from every possible angle. He adjusted the lights to a pleasant darkness, turned back the coverlet. The casket looked substantial enough to hold his modest weight, but his courage left him. He couldn't climb in. Something would tear or collapse; nothing was ever as solid as it looked. But he yearned, and he walked up and down telling himself to go ahead, and finally he got up the nerve to caress her face. At that, he realized that he was a person whose pleasure came from viewing, not touching – and he adjusted his thinking to include scorn for anyone who would stoop to defile such perfection. As closing time approached, his aesthetic passion waned and his lust took over and he masturbated into a basket of carnations, carefully, surreptitiously, without defiling.

After the funeral Billy felt older and out of place in school. There was a new sophistication about him, the kind that comes when an inner direction has been taken, even when the direction is opposed to one's admitted goals. He put on a little weight and his side whiskers sprouted, giving him a cat-like appearance that was enhanced by his round, innocent eyes. His step became a little heavier, his voice a little deeper; he was becoming more man than boy. His parents noticed the change and knew that he would be leaving soon.

His mother gave him her usual advice. "Don't be in any hurry, Billy, my son. Don't bite off more than you can chew." She had always pointed out his limitations, telling him that he would never be high off the ground but that even a little man could be respectable. "Don't get one of those loud, pushy women who try to be above everybody else. Find some nice, quiet girl who won't make your life a hell." Billy hoped she would never find out how literally he had taken her advice.

He did leave home, as expected, as soon as he finished high school and got a job as a bank teller far from home and watchful parents.

With no one to notice, he took to calling at wakes. He would check the obituaries for age and cause of death, then would choose the evening's entertainment. He signed the book, shook hands all around, and viewed the body to his heart's content, comparing it with the perfect Ida point by point. Although none came close to measuring up, an evening seemed wasted if he didn't make the search. He made no move toward the bodies; he wouldn't dream of it; he was delighted simply to enjoy the viewing and the odors and to appreciate the artistry that went into such a production. What others might call a nasty compulsion Billy considered his blessing, the special interest that gave his life its uniqueness.

This activity required a sober wardrobe. Billy began to acquire one and kept it in order, buying quiet suits and tie-handkerchief sets with a dark stripe, and sometimes blacking the soles of his shoes.

After a few years, when his father died, he switched to wearing black ties only, and when his mother followed a short time later, he added an armband. Several weeks went by and he was still wearing the armband when the head of Public Relations stopped by his cage one day and said, "Look here, Bill, the black tie we could put up with, but the armband is too much. You can't spend all your time in the vault. You have to face the public, and the public likes an upbeat image."

"Yes sir," Billy answered in a composed, toneless voice.

"The public be damned," he said later to himself. "I'll give up the armband if that son of a bitch insists, but I'm going to show proper respect for the dead no matter what First National's image is."

He went shopping. He looked first on the rack of size 38-short suits in the men's department, hoping he had grown some since last time. Then he went to the boys' department. His pride suffered, but he was determined to outwit the head of Public Relations.

"Try this one, sir," said the sales clerk. "We'll take it up for you without charge." He offered Billy a suit made from suave blend of medium blues and grays.

"That's exactly what I do not want," answered Billy, feeling his lip curl slightly. "I am in mourning," he went on. "I need something subdued."

After shopping every boy's department in town and turning down their garish garments, he hired a tailor to make him a black-on-black stripe, a black-on-black check, and a dark gray-on-black tweed for sports wear. He could tell that the head of Public Relations did not care for his choices, but since he had given up the armband, he was not criticized.

No one knew of Billy's dreams. He had no friends. Even his acquaintances were distant. His dates bore little resemblance to his fantasy, all of them being more on the loud, pushy side than the girl of his dreams.

He was well thought of, however. His neighbors called him "a nice, quiet young man, the kind you don't often see these days." At the delicatessen where he bought smoked fish on payday the manager saved cheese boxes for him, the wooden ones that stack well. He kept them in a black lacquered bookcase and filled them with the specimens he found during vacations following tips in *The Fossil Hunter's Guide* and on trips to Rushing Creek east of town, a fossil bed that had been dry for years.

He felt that cultural interests would contribute to his respectability; thus he sacrificed some of his funeral home evenings to appear at the symphony with someone from his list of ever-available women: Edith, Gertrude, Mildred and Emmaline, and if even Emmaline happened to be too busy to hear Beethoven's *Missa solemnis* with him, then Florence.

The art museum was another place he often took a date. There he would maneuver her to his favorite bench to rest her feet and view the open ironwork sculpture of a cat with a bird hanging caged inside.

He was tolerated but not loved by the women he dated, though no one could really say why, for the ones who would go out with him had no other dates for comparison. He held doors and helped them with their coats, courtly as a grandfather. He remembered their problems and asked to be brought up to date. But he was low-key among the women, even the mousiest, and though they did not know each other, if they had, they would have agreed that there was something wrong with him. No one of them could quite describe it, but together they might have found him out.

His research, for instance; he was always doing research on Caius Claudius Nero. Why would a bank teller want to research Nero? Edith and Mildred put it down as a fad, Emmaline as an irritation. Gertrude and Florence knew only that Nero was somebody in history, a fiddler, they thought. They all ignored the research and went out with Billy because of his symphony tickets – and because nobody else ever invited them.

Each, because she couldn't do any better, tolerated the distance that Billy Malkin managed to preserve. Other men took women to their apartments, or at least parked in Ordrey's Lane with a pint of whiskey; Billy parked at The Blue Tree and took his dates inside. Other men abraded the pretty, popular faces with their stubble – and went on from there; Billy never so much as tickled a cheek. But what could they complain about? It was a night out, wasn't it?

Billy lived in this quiet way, spending his days at the bank, his evenings pursuing respectability or hoping to find another Ida at some out-of-the-way mortuary. If a chasm stretched between his dreams and his day-to-day, was he so different from everyone else?

Throughout his twenties and into his thirties he had worked at the bank while one drab day followed another, seated with a calm face and a disappointed heart on a high stool in his teller's cage, occasionally climbing down long enough to escort a coupon clipper into the vault. Around the time of his thirtieth birthday he realized that he would be doing this for the rest of his life. From then on he dragged himself to work in the morning with difficulty. But he knew of no alternative, so he accepted his fate, reserving only a deeply buried hope that someday he would find his niche.

At last one evening he opened the paper to read that Allan Joseph, a local funeral director, was looking for the right young man – "sober, sympathetic, courteous" – to be his assistant. With the deeply buried hope blossoming, Billy made an appointment to be interviewed.

He spent the early morning grooming and re-grooming his person and clothing. He trimmed his whiskers and got them so short on one side that it became necessary to shave. He chose his current black-on-black striped suit and treated anything that could possibly be considered a spot, then changed his mind and went through the whole procedure again with the black-on-black check. He swabbed and spotted and steamed and pressed; he cut his nails and flossed his teeth. Finally, in the car before going in for the interview, he availed himself of several long, strengthening swallows of odorless vodka.

He needn't have worried. In Mr. Joseph's outer office he observed his competitors as they were shown in and then out again. One had long, greasy hair, another wore flashy clothes; the only one who looked appropriate had no feel for the language. Talking with the others in the outer office, he even used the word "corpse."

In the inner sanctum, Billy's feeling for the dead unfolded with increasing eloquence. Mr. Joseph did not need to persuade him that the funeral was an art form. He had discovered this for himself years earlier. As emotionally cathartic as a stage tragedy, it takes place in one's own experience, uses one's own version of the script, and best of all, casts one in a full and prominent role. It alters horror and disease and medical indignities into roses and wreaths and blankets of carnations.

Warming with the spread of vodka in his bloodstream, Billy told Mr. Joseph that the funeral, in his hometown, had been an important social event. "It reunites quarreling families and brings old friends to call, and it creates a fresh sense of closeness between the generations and people who haven't much in common." He wiped his pink, newly-shaven cheeks with a black-bordered handkerchief and rose from his chair to pace as he talked.

"It is the only event in a human life that is fully celebrated. Other events — births, and certainly weddings — are partially celebrated, of course, but the funeral is the culmination. How many friends can one expect at a birth?" he asked rhetorically. "And aren't weddings interesting only to the participants?" Inflamed by true belief and vodka, he declaimed, "At a funeral the supporting cast takes full control. The star is already out of the way. And as for the matter of celebrating — births and weddings are open questions, aren't they? One never knows what the outcome will be, thus hesitates to celebrate fully — for wouldn't it be embarrassing to endorse a wedding that will soon end in blows and divorce? At a funeral the question is settled. Anyone can speak with certainty."

Mr. Joseph made a motion as though to say something, but Billy continued, "A funeral is a man's final drama. And the funeral director is the producer of this drama, along with being stage manager, make-up man, electrician, and advisor. He is a true artist."

Billy's eloquence more than made up for his lack of training. He could take courses while he learned the business. Mr. Joseph would be happy to pay his tuition. He started work at the mortuary after a decent notice at the bank.

Billy was now happy, as only the man can be who has found his niche after years of half-hearted striving toward the wrong goals. He was friends with the dead. He liked them and liked making them nice to view, and if the untimely dead were his favorites, he did not slight those whose time was overdue. He was sympathetic and fair. Even the grotesque rested with dignity in the parlors of Allen Joseph's Mortuary.

As for Billy's personal habits, they didn't exactly change but one could say that they became infused with new spirit. His well being among the cold and still was so pronounced that he began to long, seriously, for the accessories of respectability: a wife, a nice house with space for a garden, and a child or two. He still had occasional fantasies of perfection and still dreamed his sheets wet at times, but he was growing into middle age and his lust, never strong, came over him infrequently enough to make him think he might possibly reconcile his differences. Now that he had one problem settled, he could concentrate on another.

Some months after Billy's arrival at Joseph's, an unheard-of incident occurred. On the second day of mourning for a Mrs. Fitzwiler, a diminutive blonde who had died in an auto crash on the freeway and had no one but a cousin to arrange the services, Billy ushered a lone caller, shaky and seedy enough to bear watching, into the parlor where Mrs. Fitzwiler lay.

"Fitzwiler?" the man asked. "Make sure it's Fitzwiler. I don't want to look at no strange corpses." His red-rimmed, wretched eyes demanded that the deceased be tried and true, no tricks, no surprises.

Billy escorted him to the casket where he stood for a moment silently before the lovely Mrs. Fitzwiler. Then he drew out an automatic pistol and shot her in the face, and before Billy could intervene, he shot her again, this time in the right breast.

"The bitch!" he screamed. "That two-timing bitch." His red eyes streamed tears. "She went and died before I got her!" He dropped the pistol. "Ain't nothing ever going to be right!"

Billy called for help and his voice, combined with the screams of the crazy man, brought Mr. Joseph and Judd, the gofer. Even Judd, with all his muscle, couldn't hold him alone; it took the three of them to subdue him before Billy could call the police.

"She thought she'd get away but I'll show her..." The angry howls went on and on as the squad car disappeared down the street.

The incident disturbed Billy deeply. It was more than his sense of decorum that suffered: it was more profound than that. He watched the papers hoping to read of the punishment of the defiler, the spoiler. Several times he fantasized Mrs. Fitzwiler in her casket instead of Ida, an infidelity that had never happened before. In one of the fantasies, she opened her eyes and spoke to him, asking, "Am I the one?" He couldn't answer, but the question, spoken in a suggestive rather than an inquiring tone, aroused him even further. The fantasy was one of his best: the odor of carnations was strong and Mrs. Fitzwiler had the good grace to move only a little, just enough to ask him that provocative question in a conspiratorial way.

After that, Billy began to take a different kind of interest in the women he dated. He knew that Mrs. Fitzwiler was not the one, but neither was Ida, not any longer. Ida had never moved or spoken. Mrs. Fitzwiler had done both, and he did not panic. There was hope that he could, with the one who was really the one, enjoy the further fruits of respectability.

But first he needed to find out for himself what drew other men to the breathing and heaving of women who moved. He decided on one (not one of the regulars) and made a date. At this point he was a little shy. Although he could be suave at an evening of Mozart, Billy the schemer felt clumsy. He bought the pint of whiskey and put it in the glove compartment. He took a trial run out to Ordrey's Lane to make sure there were no mud holes.

After a porterhouse and a bottle of hearty burgundy at the Steer

Room and a movie at The Big Red X, he drove Nelly out to Ordrey's Lane. By dome light he poured her a drink of the whiskey into a flowered foam cup.

"You scared of germs, or what?" she asked.

"I just thought you'd like a cup."

He caught a thread in the zipper of her dress. It would go neither up nor down, and Nelly did not offer to help. He worked on it without pleasure, and when it finally yielded, he discovered that her body smelled not floral and delicate, but salty, yeasty and ultimately sweaty. He zipped her back up and drove her home, his investment notwithstanding.

All the ground he'd gained with Mrs. Fitzwiler was lost with Nelly. His fantasy slunk back to Ida, who seemed to care neither that he'd gone nor that he'd returned.

One day a call came to Joseph's for the ambulance service that was part of the business. Billy rode along with Judd and listened to Judd chatter as he drove. "We've had calls from this one before. She's a cripple, falls once in a while, and needs a ride to the hospital."

The young woman sat, naked, on the bare floor of the cluttered apartment. Brown glass fragments were scattered around her in a drying puddle of stale-smelling beer. Music boomed from speakers mounted on the wall.

"Hi, Mermaid," said Judd, tossing his cap toward the bed. "How'd it happen this time?"

"Would you mind turning the music down?" she said. "It doesn't do a thing for this scene."

Judd found the control and switched it off.

"And bring me a wet washrag out of the bathroom?"

Billy jumped ahead of Judd and let the water run warm before soaking the washcloth. The bathroom wall was crammed to the corners with unframed paintings, nudes, all of them. Leaving these startling images, Billy, thoroughly rattled, carried the dripping washcloth out to the young woman, who seemed unbowed by her afflictions.

"What the hell happened?" asked Judd again.

She wiped the blood off her arm before speaking. "How about bringing me that striped blanket off the bed?" she asked.

When her nakedness was covered and the glass swept aside, Linnet told them. "I was just getting into the beat, and my beer bottle shimmied right out of my hand. When I grabbed for it, I fell, myself. I landed on this shoulder," she said, reaching to probe it. "It's probably just a sprain, but I'd better get it x-rayed. I can't get around without a shoulder. It's a good thing the phone is right here or they wouldn't have found me till I stunk." She did not mention why she happened to be naked.

"I'll carry her," said Billy quickly. "We don't need the stretcher."

Judd gave him a look but said nothing.

Linnet put her good arm around Billy's neck and winced when he picked her up, but Billy did not volunteer the stretcher. Her body was small, no bigger than a child's, and her crinkly-curly hair was yellow. Billy glanced at her lifeless legs peeking out at the knee from the striped blanket.

The breeze from the open door set off wind chimes, flat shells tinkling in a cool, disordered way like strangers whispering secrets.

Linnet was solidly light in his arms through the hall, past pressed wildflowers and books and a long mural in red-painted strings showing miles of electric wire on pylons, a voltage garden. Billy kept his gaze away from these images. He watched the floor, and occasionally he glanced at her unmoving knees almost hidden in the blanket.

Outside, Billy walked slowly to the hearse. On the way to the hospital he rode in back with Linnet while Judd drove. She closed her eyes and breathed as though attending to pain. He watched her legs under the blanket. When her eyes opened, she caught him. "It's not polite to stare at a cripple's legs."

"I'm sorry." His face swelled.

Linnet was kept in the hospital overnight and then another night when her temperature rose. Billy called on her immediately. He also sent flowers, carnations that turned out to be red and odorless despite his instructions. The next day he brought her, on impulse, a sack of jellybeans. On the third day he drove her home, having learned a great deal about her life: how she had injured her spine, how she painted, read, played the flute, went out with friends.

His own life would have to change. It was sterile by comparison:

he could see how lifeless a life he really had. He would learn. He must! She must never know what he was really like. New interests: piano, sports, a reading program. He would jog, or take up yoga. She would see that he too had worth.

His first new interest was Linnet herself.

They went for drives in the country to follow the spring. They watched the late movies together. He took her to hear Mozart's *Requiem* and to see the sculpture of the cat with the bird caged inside. She in turn took him to a jazz joint and a sidewalk art fair. They talked endlessly. About Life and about Death (Billy careful not to commit himself) and about everything in between, and especially about Marriage, each one denying interest.

On a summer Sunday, after a picnic, Linnet lay in the sun with her hair down loose over her shirt. Billy lay beside her. Covertly he watched her legs tumbled crazily one over the other in the grass. Ants walked on her skin. She did not brush them off. "Don't you feel those ants?" he asked, wondering just how dead those legs of hers were.

"Yes," she said, looking at two ants walking over her forearm. "They feel good."

He closed his eyes. An ant crawled on his neck. He twitched, then tried to go limp and enjoy it. It crawled down his collar to the soft flesh near his underarm. It didn't feel good to him. He started to cringe, took a deep breath, and thought about the six legs of the ant wading through perspiration. Was the perspiration ankle deep or knee deep? Did ants have knees? Bees did, didn't they?

Linnet rolled over on him and kissed him. He waited, unable to go limp, feeling overwhelmed. The ant was one thing: it could be put aside by thought, but Linnet?

He pressed against her, then allowed himself to touch her waist, her hips. His hand moved to her leg, but it was warm. He panicked.

He opened his eyes and rolled her away. An ant was crawling on her shirt.

"Is it because I'm crippled?" she asked. Her eyes reddened.

"No! Absolutely not!" He pulled two clover blossoms and tied the stems together. He stroked her tangled hair and tucked the flowers behind her ear, then stood up. "Let's go home."

He did not phone her the next evening. Instead he went to the library. When he walked past the desk, the librarian called out to him, "Mr. Malkin, we have a new book for you." She pulled the book from the shelf behind her. "There's a long section about Nero in it." The title was *Perversions in Famous Men*. He snatched two more books at random and hurriedly checked out all three.

At home he went to bed early. He shivered and pulled up the cover. Some time near dawn he sat up and read about Nero – the butchered children, the orgies, and about the other perversions as well, weeping as he read, with rage and sick fascination fighting for his heart.

Hours later the phone woke him. "Are you okay?" Mr. Joseph asked.

"I've got a touch of flu," Billy answered.

"Take care of yourself. You've got to watch those things. Don't want to pass on germs to the customers." He chuckled at his little inside joke.

Billy hung up. It was the wrong joke for him just now. He dressed quickly and went out.

As he passed the deli, the manager called out the open door, "Mr. Malkin, don't you want these boxes?" Billy bought a raspberry Danish and accepted the boxes along with reproof for having abandoned his old habits. Several blocks later he dropped boxes and Danish in a trash barrel.

Through one neighborhood, then another and another, he headed away from downtown. At the river he crossed and walked along a footpath choked with roots and runners near the water's edge. Three ducks paddled along in front of him. He wished he'd kept the Danish to offer them. Then he became aware of how long ago he'd last eaten, and he wished he'd kept the Danish for himself.

It was well into evening. He had been walking since early afternoon. On his way home he heard the sounds of children's evening games and mothers' voices calling them home. Would he, the perverted, ever have the home, the children, the evening sounds?

He argued with himself about love. Love wasn't the problem, he decided. His capacity for love was not great, but to the extent that he could, he loved Linnet. It was this other thing.

Linnet seemed to think it was because there was something wrong with her. Well, there was, wasn't there?

His heels were blistered. He took his shoes off and walked barefoot the rest of the way home, wincing at every pebble that touched his soft feet but feeling the kind of triumph that worshipers must feel when they climb miles of stone steps on their knees.

The phone was ringing. "What do I have to do, sprain my other shoulder?"

During the two weeks before the wedding, Billy stayed busy. He bought two pairs of pajamas, ten shares of the mutual fund listed safest that week and a life insurance policy. He cleaned his apartment, threw away his fossils and installed hand rails in the bath. He took a blood test, got a haircut, bought a marriage license and contacted a minister. He took his books back to the library and put his Nero notes in a lock box, just in case. Then, feeling like a born-again in the light summer suit that Linnet had suggested, he met his bride in her wheelchair in front of the minister's cold summer fireplace.

"Do you take this woman...?" the minister asked solemnly.

"I do," he heard his own voice reply. It sounded composed and respectable.

On their way to the honeymoon resort they talked shyly about the weather and listened to the radio and thought their own thoughts. Billy well knew that their courtship had not conformed to the modern model depicted everywhere he looked. But whose did, when scrutinized? Nothing was perfect. If he was old-fashioned, so be it. Linnet hadn't complained, had she? Only the once, him panicking, when she acted, well, pushy.

At the resort, Billy made certain arrangements. Then they toured the attractions and dined leisurely, Billy consulting his watch from time to time. At last, after dessert and then cordials, the appointed time had come. Their private moments would be put off no longer.

Billy had planned carefully, and no sooner had they settled into their room than there was a soft rap on the door. "Mr. Malkin?" asked the delivery boy. "Flowers for the lady." He set an enormous gray vase of white carnations on a table near the door. "Goodnight."

"Beautiful!" cried Linnet.

Billy moved them to the bedside table and buried his face, inhaling deeply, before he carried Linnet from her chair and placed her carefully in the bed.

"Billy," she asked, "how did you know I was the one for you?"

He took a carnation from the vase and put in her hair, then another and another. "I don't know," he answered finally. When her hair was fully decorated, he laid her back into the pillows, arranged her legs, and climbed on the bed himself. "I don't know, but you're about as close to perfection as a woman could be." With his face near her hair, each deep breath drew in the spicy odor. He shifted so that his body was on top of hers.

She moved. "Billy, don't you want to know why I chose you?"

Startled, he pulled back. The question had never occurred to him. Then he groaned and buried his face in the flowers tangled in her hair. "Don't move," he whispered. His weight pushed her deeper into the pillows. "Please don't move."

.∧.∧.∧.∧.∧.

Change at the Fortune Cookie Plant

I could always quit. But I'm in charge, and if I didn't take care of things here, no one else would, and then where would I be? Always I Ching tells me: "THE SUPERIOR ONE DOES NOT PERMIT THOUGHTS TO GO BEYOND SITUATION," and "PERSEVERANCE FURTHERS."

Where would I be? Without the plant, where would I be? I see myself alone and lost on a dark chilly street, hungry. One of those pathetic hags who wrap themselves in bigger women's coats and sleep on the grating of a steam vent or in a cardboard box in the park. I'd eat at the soup kitchen, wash at the library, accept the Salvation Army's prayers.

But I'd certainly like, if not to quit, at least to make some changes. Being in charge ought to mean that I could do what I want, shouldn't it? But even though the folks are dead, it's still their business.

I do know the operation. I suppose that's a plus. I've spent my entire career here, my entire life, starting as a baby coming in with my parents. I can't remember a time when I wasn't part of the family business.

The plant has always had two divisions: dough and fortunes. My mother, of course, was in charge of dough, the female thing, and my father did fortunes. This division was not harmonious. Each one wanted to boss the other's area; each one took me aside time and again to point out the other's irresponsibility. My father thought Mother intentionally put too much sugar in the dough, a waste that added up, he said, and Mother thought he was miserly with the fortunes to spite her, using the same ones over and over, too damned

stingy to build the Fortune Research Department into what it ought
to be.

When I took over, I cut down on sugar, and I connected Fortune
Research to the Library of Congress' database, thus bringing to our
fingertips the accumulated wisdom of Western civilization. But
these changes merely enhanced the operation as it stood; they did
not touch the root of my dissatisfaction.

If it hadn't been for my fear as a small child of the steam vents that
would be my parents' bed and thus mine if anything happened to the
Factory, I would have enjoyed my long apprenticeship. Even afraid
as I was, I did occasionally indulge myself, snitch scraps of dough
without the worry of meeting production. I found that I could
arrange certain fortunes if I worked fast and looked angelic. I was responsible, for instance, for "YOUR CHILDREN ARE NOT YOUR
CHILDREN," from *The Prophet,* that caused all the commotion with
the redneck and his wife at the House of Lotus. I've always enjoyed
doing fortunes. But my parents almost split up over the trouble at the
House of Lotus and I had to give up the good times. They warned
me that a fortune cookie is supposed to be a harmless message
wrapped in sweet, bland dough.

When I first took over the plant, I made a clean sweep of my parents' rules, which were senselessly contradictory. I rewrote the man-
ual. But rules have lives of their own, and they don't like being swept
aside. They get their hooks in, and they suck out your vital juices.
They all came back, sneaked in one at a time, and jostled among the
new ones. I can't move without stumbling over rules. Since I've been
in charge, I've spent a lot of time pondering: Is this the right way to
operate? Is that? Which is better? If I follow this rule, I break that
one, and I always worry about the one I've broken. And rules never
tell you what you need to know to make important things go your
way. They only tell you how to keep things the way they are.

Since the knock-down and drag-out at the House of Lotus, our
buyer has wanted to see the product, which means each and every
fortune, before he buys. We have to compose what his customer is
going to want, which I think should be a straightforward and well put
together fortune, the truthful fortune that will illuminate the path,

right? "YOUR CHILDREN ARE NOT YOUR CHILDREN." But no, at the House of Lotus the manager is concerned with "real world" and "bottom line" and what he says goes. "No," he says. "No funny business. You think I want my customer to choke? To sue? To spit the cookie on the tablecloth?" The manager's the one who decides whether or not our product is delivered to the person it belongs to. It's no way to run a business, but that's how it crumbles, like it or not. My father knew that the real world is harsh. He did his own censoring. The manager does mine.

But I've gotten off the subject.

As I said, I resent having to be in charge. It's cracked up to be an honor. My mother insisted that I was lucky. I've risen in the world. Not everyone makes it. There are bag ladies all over the place. I have an education, I own a portfolio, I blow-dry my hair and wear a skirt and heels from morning till night. What this means is that I have to support my alma mater and make her proud of me. I have to clutch my portfolio through Augusts and Octobers. I have to wear heels and get bunions and then jog on them for my figure's sake, because I'm the one in charge of the cookie plant and I ought to present a good corporate image.

And if I neglect these obligations? Then the imps and demons come in the night to drag me off to the torture room. "You're the one who rose in the world," they jeer. "Would you rather fall?" They sting me for my omissions, and because there are so many rules, there are a great many omissions.

So I work on corporate image for a while, only my heart's not in it and soon I start to get shabby. My heels run over, the skirt gets stained with cookie dough, I let my hair go wild. I say to myself, well, if you're not going to be Miss America, you can at least pay attention to the portfolio. I work on it for a while, buy mutuals, sell Ginnie Maes, but my heart's not in that either. I'm not one of the big boys. Then I shiver and remember that I've neglected to make my alma mater proud of me. This task is hopeless, and it's a waste of time to try, so I go back to corporate image and the cycle starts over. In the meantime, I run the cookie plant.

You see, this business is easy. I can run it with my hands tied. An innocuous message wrapped in a twisted piece of sweet dough. Tours come through the plant. Busloads of tourists, foreigners, singles, Elderhostel, inmates of all kinds. I remember one particular group of school children that toured the plant years ago when I was small. Little ones, kindergarten, maybe. Just the right age for this kind of place. Little girls with pigtails like mine, holding their chins up and sniffing the aroma of baking cookies. I melted right into the group, toured the plant, sampled the cookies, giggled over the fortunes, and when they left, I howled, because they were free to go out in the world and find uncensored fortunes, while I was already shackled here.

Tourists love the aroma. I'm so lucky, they tell me, to work in a place that smells this good. And they admire the Fortune Research Department. Not only are we hooked up to the Library of Congress, but we're also working on access to *TianMa* software that will put us in touch with the accumulated wisdom of the East. With so much at my disposal, people envy me.

A friend suggested that instead of quitting I expand the business. Cookie valentines, perhaps. I did a valentine once. It was a great red heart-shaped cookie, and the message inside was this:

Just as long as you'll be true
That's as long as I'll love you
But should you fail to toe the line
I'll find another Valentine.

It was truthful. It was straightforward. It even illuminated the path, but you can imagine how well it sold among the Hallmarks.

How about "Cookies by Fax"? When my thoughts stray beyond my situation, this is my dream. I strike a key at the terminal here at the plant, thus activating a randomizer so that everything is left to chance, and a fortune comes into being. After the briefest lull, the machinery on the desk of the manager at the House of Lotus responds: first the computer flashes its mysterious disk lights, then a pair of rollers shapes the dough, a message slides out of the Whisperjet, and finally, after thirty seconds in the desktop oven, presto! his morning fortune, printed in Chinese characters by *TianMa*, awaits his pleasure: straight from Chi'en, The Creative, "NINE AT THE TOP

MEANS: ARROGANT DRAGON WILL HAVE CAUSE TO REPENT." A triumphant marriage of hardware and software. The only trouble with this victory is that the manager has never heard of I Ching, and he cannot read Chinese.

But wait. My mind's eye sees another fortune landing on his desk: "YOU WILL SOON BE GUIDED, MATERIALLY AND SPIRITUALLY, INTO HIGHER EDUCATION." Maybe he could still learn Chinese. But this is my father, no doubt, modifying from the grave, giving the manager his Pablum to take the edge off my zingers. Even Cookies by Fax will feel the influence of the censor.

Actually, Cookies by Fax will probably never be developed. My fortunes advise against such an experiment. "BE EVER THE LAST TO GO OVER A DEEP RIVER," says the Spanish proverb. "THE CAUTIOUS SELDOM MAKE MISTAKES," agrees Confucious. The only part I could experiment with risk-free would be dough, and that doesn't interest me. What earthly good would there be to offering fancy-shaped fortune cookies? Chocolate ones? Coconut? Bubble gum? No, I'm not going to contribute to choices that simply take people's time and throw them off the track. They don't pay enough attention to the fortune as it is; a fortune is the easiest thing in the world to neglect.

The truth is that what I know about maintaining the present operation is my security. I know how to keep things from happening. I catch a whiff of sulfur, and I know there's a bad egg in the batch; I throw it out before something happens. There's a scritch in the dough roller and I call the mechanics before trouble starts. The fellows in Fortune Selection laugh a little too loudly, and I pull the run and look for the jokes. People don't like jokes on top of their chop suey and Mandarin duck. The manager has told me so time and again. They don't want an incendiary fortune that says, "LOOK TO THE FUTURE; THERE IS NO PRESENT," and burns up in their fingers. I pull out the funny stuff, just as my father did, even though I like it best. This very morning I had to reprimand one of the selectors for playing around with Tennyson in my morning cookie: "THE OLD ORDER CHANGETH, YIELDING PLACE TO NEW."

So here I am, in charge of the fortune cookie plant. But in spite of the censor, I'm feeling an inexplicable tension ready to snap. What about that old order changing? What about its yielding place to new?

I'm feeling an irresistible urge to turn some tables, to goad my alma mater into teaching Chinese, to gamble my portfolio on Cookies by Fax research. This could be the day. So I'll open another cookie. Take advice wherever you can get it.

"EVERYTHING ACTS TO FURTHER. NO BLAME."

.\.\.\.\.\

The Other Real World

When the new mother had healed enough from the shock of the double birth to take the baby home from the hospital, she took the bear cub as well. They urged her to put him in a zoo, where a mother bear might adopt and nurse him. But the cub was her flesh and blood, just as the baby was, and she was going to keep him, difficult as it might be.

She dressed them like twins for a week or so: little shirts and diapers, knit gowns, bibs. But the cub had his own garment: soft bear fur was all he needed. So the baby got the wardrobe and the cub was allowed to be a bear.

She continued to care for them equally, however, and they both thrived. They slept in the room where she worked sewing shirt seams for the factory, the cub in a warm den under the baby's crib. As the months went by and the twins grew, the bars between them posed less and less of a barrier. First the bear learned to climb *in*, then the baby to climb *out*. Inside the crib they played with the rattles, the stuffed animals, the musical mobile that swung from the headboard. On the floor they played with the ball, the blocks, the rocking horse, and the chicken that clucked when dragged across the floor, all to the background hum of their mother's sewing machine.

One toy, however, that the bear failed to enjoy was the tall mirror attached to the door. The baby would look in it and smile, enchanted by her own image, while the bear smelled it and batted it with a paw, treating it like an inanimate piece of glass and growling to draw the baby's attention back to where he felt it belonged, on him.

"How fortunate!" thought their mother. "Most little girls have no bear twin to remind them that the mirror isn't everything." And she took the big mirror away and substituted a small one.

The mother had an old fur coat of *her* mother's, shabby and disreputable, that she wore sometimes when she walked alone in the woods near her home. A coat to withdraw in, one for animal warmth, not human gaze. She pushed the twins into the woods in a double stroller. The path was just wide enough to accommodate them, no wider. No one else was ever there. The woman and her children had the whole woods to themselves.

"How fortunate!" she thought again. Taking the children in the stroller through the neighborhood had never been a rewarding experience. In the neighborhood they were on display, but in the woods they could be themselves.

The entrance to the woods was always the same, through a gate in the stone wall that encircled the small wild area in the midst of suburban sprawl, a little section of green saved from the endless shopping malls and tract houses. But once inside, the woman noticed that the path was different from one day to the next. At first she attributed the changes to her unfamiliarity with the woods, but after enough walks, she realized that something else was involved, something she couldn't quite grasp.

For one thing, the woods grew larger. The path that took half an hour to travel the first time now stretched far enough to take half a day. "And I'm not walking any more slowly," she thought.

The food she found in the woods changed too. On the first day she ate two ripe thimbleberries, and that was all she found. But as the walk got longer, more food appeared. There was no need to bring a lunch. The picnic was already there, spread out for the taking. Not just thimbleberries, though the bear liked them a lot, but fresh fish as well, cooking in a small fire pit just off the path, or a hot round loaf of bread which she could smell baking in a hive-shaped oven. There was milk for the children and wine for herself, cooling in jugs submerged in a shaded stream.

At first she did not take any, thinking the food belonged to someone else. But one day she had neglected to eat breakfast and was very hungry. The bread smelled wonderful. "Just a bite," she thought, and helped herself. One bite led to another, as usual, and of course she had to give some to her daughter and the bear. Soon the loaf was gone.

"I can't believe I really did that," she said to herself, ashamed. "I've become a thief." But by then the hive-shaped oven was once again redolent of baking bread. Another loaf had taken the place of what she'd eaten.

"This is a miracle," she thought. "If I hadn't given birth to the bear as well as the child, I'd have never found this place where food replenishes itself as soon as it's consumed. I'd have stayed home or gone to the mall. I'd have been just another vain, unhappy consumer, and so would my daughter."

She continued to spend her spare time in the woods. As she did so, the woods continued to grow. At last she realized that the woods was no longer just a token scrap of green within the sprawl of civilization. It now covered enough territory so that the suburb was small by comparison. "This is more like it," she thought.

But one evening a member of the Community Council came knocking at her door. He was inquiring of all citizens how they spent their time. "What contribution are you making to society?" he asked. He left a questionnaire.

She pondered the question as she sewed that night. What contribution *was* she making? Wasn't she spending her time selfishly? Doing what she pleased instead of what she ought to do? She was avoiding the trap of the mirror and the shopping mall, but what was she doing for society?

The next day she stayed home from the woods and filled out the questionnaire. The twins played in the kitchen. The little girl whined to be taken out, and the cub left droppings on the floor. But that was the price she'd have to pay, she thought, to be a better citizen. When her phone rang and she was asked to help support a Community Council candidate, one who promised to be more responsive to the citizens' wishes, she involved herself in the campaign.

It was exciting to feel she could make a difference. Being part of the group made her feel useful. Yes, she had to spend more time at the shopping mall, for that's where Campaign Headquarters was located. And yes, she had to spend more time at the mirror, because looks counted at the mall. But it was the campaign that mattered, and she could afford to make some sacrifices for that.

She took the child with her to play with the other children while she worked. The bear, of course, had to stay at home. He didn't behave well alone, and she had to build him a pen.

"That's the price you have to pay for good government," she thought. For citizen involvement. It was too bad. She missed the woods, the happiness of the bear, but what right did she have to these luxuries when the society was going to hell? How could she abdicate her responsibilities as a citizen? How could she leave the town in a mess for her child to grow up in?

She did worry about the bear. It paced its pen and growled when she approached to toss in its food. She promised herself that she would do better by the bear as soon as she had more time.

Her candidate won. The victory party lasted late. Wine was drunk. The thought did come to her, as she was sipping a glass of it, that the wine from the jugs in the stream in the woods had been better. Much better. And it hadn't left her hung over.

But such thoughts were elitist, weren't they? What right did she have to fine wine?

The new Community Council settled in. Meetings were held. Bills were passed. Citizens wrote letters to the editor. The business of the suburb went on. Yes, there were changes. Permission to build the ten-story hotel was refused. But when the developers scaled down their project and a compromise was reached, a five-story office building went up on a slightly larger site.

There was time now for the woman to go back to the woods. She could spend a little time strolling on the ever-changing path, feasting on the picnic there for the taking. But her daughter whined at the prospect. "I want to go to the mall," she cried. "My friends all go to the mall." "Already the girl says this, so young!" thought the mother. And the bear had become so dangerous that she dared not let him out of his pen. He might go on a rampage and maul somebody. She would have to walk in the woods alone.

The gate was just as she remembered it. She entered. Trees

arched over the path. The peace of the woods embraced her. She walked, rejoicing, her shabby fur coat wrapped around her. She wondered what she would find to eat. She walked on. But after twenty minutes she was back at the gate. The woods had shrunk. She had found nothing at all to eat.

"Could I have been mistaken about the woods?" she asked herself. She stood there by the entrance, hating to leave, feeling deprived. Her gaze fell on a thicket. One ripe thimbleberry hung crimson on a branch. "No," she thought, "I wasn't mistaken. This is real, as real as anything there is." She popped the thimbleberry into her mouth and fitted it over the end of her tongue like a cap.

But the woods had definitely shrunk. She hadn't spent half an hour on the path before coming to the end of it. The suburb had squeezed it smaller and smaller. What a pity! She would have to speak to the Community Council. After all she'd done for her candidate, he ought to represent her and take her concerns seriously.

He spoke kindly to her. "There, there," he said. "I'm sorry you're so upset. But this is the real world. Progress is progress."

She understood. Nothing could be done. The Community Council would be no help. The real world was the real world, and progress was progress. The candidate was helpless against it. Her spirits were very low.

That night before going to sleep, she prayed for the first time since childhood. "I need help," she prayed. "Somebody help me, please." She didn't really believe in God anymore, but she needed to pray anyway. "What can I do?" she asked. "My daughter is lost to the shopping mall, the bear is too dangerous to let out of his pen, and the woods have shrunk alarmingly."

After a time she awoke, thinking that she'd been dreaming she was standing near the stream in the woods. The jugs were cooling in the water. The hive-shaped oven sent forth its aroma. The fresh fish sizzled on a circle of firestones. Someone was standing nearby holding a high-powered flashlight, the beam of which penetrated the darkness of the woods. She saw a pattern of stones that looked like the foundation of some kind of structure, but she couldn't tell what it was. Then she heard a voice. "The real world is the real world," it said. She glared angrily. She'd heard those words before. But the voice spoke again. "All you have to do is come here," it said. "The forest is real, but only if you come."

She felt the hairs on her arms lift. She also felt dizzy from the view, the view she was glimpsing of a real world dependent upon her attendance. If she did *not* go there, it would disappear, perhaps disappear entirely.

But so would the shopping mall. If nobody went there, it would cease to be real.

What about my daughter, she wondered.

"Your daughter will find the woods herself some day," came the answer. "If she's so inclined."

"And the bear?"

"Open the pen." This voice from within sounded authentic. It certainly carried more authority than the voice of her candidate, who could come up with nothing better than "There, there," and "Progress is progress." She opened the pen.

The bear shambled out and disappeared into the woods. In her future visits she would sometimes hear him crash around in the underbrush, and once she saw him raking thimbleberries off the stalks.

Again she attended the woods daily, only now she did more than stroll. Sometimes she saw the foundation of the structure again, where new stones appeared from time to time. Sometimes she sensed the presence of someone else, and was able to converse with the voice she had heard. There was always food nearby.

When the call came for her to return to the campaign, her answer was ready. "No," she said. "That's not the best use of my time."

"What about your contribution?" This question again, the one that had led to her losses.

"I am making a different contribution," she said. "The real world is the real world." Far too many people already were making the candidate's world real; her contribution was to attend to the other world she had found.

The candidate was angry and critical. She was no longer useful to him and therefore would be disregarded.

But she'd already paid the price of leaving the woods. This time she would pay the price of finding it again. Every choice requires a sacrifice.

Months and years went by. The woman continued her attendance to the woods. The stone structure grew higher. Her old coat grew more and more shabby.

The home she made for her daughter kept her involved with the community as well. People continued to ask her to make a contribution, to back a candidate or work on a committee. Occasionally she found community work that did not violate her commitment to what she began to call "sylvanaculture" for lack of a better term. This put her in contact with others interested in things besides the mirror and the shopping mall. She made connections.

One day the daughter of her old Community Council candidate came to visit. What she wanted was not clear at first. "I've heard about you," the girl said. "I think you're the one who can help me." They talked a little, about one thing and another, and then she got down to the point. "I dreamed I gave birth to twins," she said. "And one of them was a seal pup."

The woman nodded. "Yes," she said. "Maybe I can help you. I'll meet you tomorrow and we'll talk. But there's a special place you'll have to go," she said. "I can show you the entrance, but you'll have to go inside alone. We'll meet there tomorrow."

"Where?" asked the girl, eyeing the woman's berry-stained fingers. "In the woods?"

"No," answered the woman. "On the beach."

∧.∧.∧.∧.∧

Melanchthon and the Process Server

Sixty-five people live in my house, none invited, none made comfortable with fresh linens and a place to hang a toothbrush, only one welcome and he the most tenuous of all. Many of them come seeking solace from the weather or their commitments and they leave when the weather changes or their commitments catch up with them. Sometimes one faction steps to the forefront and demands my attention, sometimes another. A few have been here since before I can remember. I have no control over their movements.

Two of the sixty-five are my parents. Though they are supposedly retired, they continue to interfere with my life and boss the house. They are old and their worst tendencies have taken them over. They quarrel, making lists of each others' faults, bitter lists, and instruct the members of the household in how they ought to behave, yet never agree on what proper behavior is. My father built the house, a sturdy fieldstone cottage, as a wedding gift for my mother. He points out its features and her lack of appreciation each time a newcomer arrives and at other times as well. My mother ignores his recitations and hums the threads of wisdom she learned as a girl. She sings in a clear voice about the way of the world, the evil and necessity of money and men. She tries to comfort me, about to bear another child without yet having found a proper father for it, but her comfort is an accusation.

My father brushes ash from the stones of the hearth and grumbles about the sloppiness of the young, which means me, and their sluttish ways, which also means me. He stands every morning, as the sun comes up, and intones the message of the day which he reads from the stained glass spider web window over the door. Long ago he built

169

the hearth, hoisting the heavy stones into place with strength and cunning, and the spider web window, staining and placing each morsel of glass with fingers directed by the god within him. My father was a mighty man when he was young.

The spider web window is magnificent, fit for a cathedral, an oval held by eight silver guy wires. The scene in it changes with the cycles, with the winds and tides, with the solstices. Newcomers are impressed and rise early to hear my father's morning reading. My own reading is far from my father's: he sees riot yielding to rot, and approaching dust storms; he sees ashes sifting down to cover the world, while I have seen since last Friday nothing but ducks – ducks swimming, ducks falling from the sky, ducks grooming themselves and preening, ducks laying eggs, ducks taking flight. I tell no one of my window readings.

And there is no one to tell. Certainly not my parents, nor these people who live here. As I said, not one of the sixty-five was invited. The ones I invite never come – only these rag-tags who struggle through the snow or the desperate sunlight to reach my house which is strong but not adequate for such numbers. It is a great disappointment. I compare these people with the ones I invite, significant people who receive well-worded invitations. "Dear Gov. So-and-So," I write, (or "Dr." or "Pres." or "Hon.") "It brings me great pleasure to offer you the comfort of my home over the holidays," etc., ending with my best wishes for their continued good fortune. But my invitations are not acknowledged and my situation grows more urgent with each day.

Oh, if only I could find a proper father for my child before he is born! I sleep with each newcomer, hoping to add his qualities to the heritage of my child, but these people are not the kind I want. There is no richness, nothing but a dribble of mediocrity leaking out in their pathetic semen.

Only the newest, upon whom I dare not place my hopes... But he will go, just as the others do, when he is ready; I have no control.

He came last Friday, trudging through the snow, carrying a half-carved wooden duck, and asked if he might hang his hammock between the two large fir trees outside. I could not allow this, could not stand him swaying in the gale all shivering and plastered white. Besides, his quality of daring made me wish him indoors to father my child. I instructed him to swing his hammock between the beams over my hearth.

That night I climbed one of the anchor ropes to his hammock, my awkward body nearly dumping us on the stones. My mother screamed when she saw me climbing. She rushed to cut the rope, but was held back by the others.

I learned this newcomer's name when the process server came looking for him. He had been giving my cottage as his address all over the country for months. He said, when I later demanded an explanation of these liberties, that he had known only that such a place had to exist; was it really the address of this house? "I must belong here, then, mustn't I?" Perhaps he must.

The process server knocked loudly and stamped snow off his boots. "Melanchthon's residence?" he asked. "I'm looking for a man named Melanchthon."

"There are sixty-four people in this house," I answered. "I know only a few by name, and none by that name. Why do you want him?"

"His wife wants him to bring their five children some supper."

"Poor babies," I said. "Come in, won't you?" He looked like an official and dutiful father for my child, and, God knows, every child needs one of those. "Have some soup. Maybe we can send some to the babies. It isn't much but it keeps us all healthy."

The process server came in and I gave him the soup. He ate heartily and invited himself to stay, promising to make repairs around the cottage in return for his daily soup and a place to sleep. They all commit themselves in that way when they come, one offering to prune the trees, another to put fresh mortar between the hearth stones, each one to bring a daily contribution to the soup.

"There's always soup, but I can't give you a bed," I said. "There are no beds available."

"That's all right," he said. "I'll put a pallet on the floor."

"That's what they all do," I answered. "And there are more people here than there is floor. My parents sleep in the only bed." I warned him just as I had warned the others.

But he insisted that he would be more comfortable here than anywhere else and would find enough space for his pallet somehow. "This is the house of my dreams," he said. "What a fireplace! What a window! Why, that window is a miracle. It ought to be in a cathedral."

The process server talked too much but I closed my ears and took him for one of my child's fathers anyway.

Later I asked him about the man he had named. "He has thin lips and except for his eyes he looks austere," he answered.

"Many people look austere. Who can identify a man by such a description?"

"Also he is selfish, childish, and demanding."

I nodded. No wonder I couldn't recognize him. His wife had given the description.

The process server was speaking again. "This man, Melanchthon, carves ducks."

Carves ducks? So that was his name — the one whose hammock had swayed and shook and started to split as we fought for our pleasure. The welcome one, for an obscure reason I cannot explain: he hasn't the title of "Pres." or "Dr." or "Hon." The process server didn't even call him "Mr."

Perhaps it has to do with truth. There is something irresistible about truth — and I have had so little of it in my life. Melanchthon reminds me of the child who said the emperor had no clothes on. Here is an example:

In my house it is the daily soup, not the bread, that is prayed for each morning and thanked for each evening. The soup is always there, simmering in the black kettle over the fire, ready for a hungry soup-eater. Each person brings food from whatever source he can find. I stir in more water and my own seasonings, using recipes given me by my mother before she became difficult. I know the soup for what it is, and privately I call it "garbage soup." But my mother will not permit such honesty: "It's all we have," she says, "and we have to make it sound appetizing." So, to the rest of them, I call it "soup du jour."

Last night the soup had no new contributions — it had been a bad day for foraging, snowy and blustering, and in the city people waited till late to put their garbage out. I added water and strengthened the seasoning and when Melanchthon tasted it, he smiled his quick, bold smile and said it tasted to him like "soup du yester-jour" and if we couldn't do any better than that, he was going to quit praying and build a greenhouse. He looked at me accusingly. "Why don't you ever make a salad, anyway?"

"Because soup is my talent," I flashed back, angry. Then I challenged him. "I'll make a salad when you make a salad bowl."

He smiled again behind his pointed beard and said, "All we ever have around here is garbage soup," but he continued to eat in spite of his complaints.

Melanchthon can be direct, and that is as near as anyone comes to truth. Perhaps this is his appeal.

He came home while the process server was sleeping. I called him by name and spoke to him about the liberties he had taken with my address.

"Melanchthon, you used my address as your own. That was not true. An address is a simple thing: the number, street, town, state and zipcode of the house you live in. You ought not to have given mine." I started to go on and lecture him upon the value of truth, the degree of correlation between the word and the thing, but he was not listening.

"You've been sleeping with the process server," he said. "Your mind's all numbers. You're saying that matter is prior to mind, that the thing exists and the word must be found to approximate it. Nonsense. Either can be prior or better still, both can exist simultaneously. The thing must just as often be found to match the word. Didn't God in His wisdom say, 'Let there be light,' before there was a Times Square? Does not each man have a bit of God in him? My address is the word for where I belong, and I thought it before I found it. Isn't that truth too?"

I argued. "Your address is where your mail is delivered. It's where the process server comes when he's looking for you."

"Exactly!" he answered. "Such an address tallies one up. Give it and you're finished."

I gave up. There was no arguing with Melanchthon about truth. "What about your hungry babies and your wife?" I asked, changing the subject.

"She wants me to support her," he said, "but I'm not going to do it." He went on. "Why should I do it just because she wants it done?"

"But the babies?"

"They aren't babies. They're lazy oafs looking for a handout. She makes it sound pathetic but it's not, it's disgusting."

"Children need care and attention and proper food if they're not to grow up warped."

Melanchthon was indifferent. "If someone wants to nurture them, let them be nurtured. If no one does, let them be warped. What does being warped mean, anyway? It takes all kinds. What if every weed on earth were nurtured into a hothouse plant? Where then would we find lilies of the field to consider?"

I decided that I would nurture even if he wouldn't and that the children would get some of our soup each day. But I brought up the argument again anyway saying, "Every child needs a father."

"Every child needs lots of fathers," he answered, and that was the end of the conversation. Besides, it was time for the singing to begin.

After dinner we sit around the hearth and sing the old songs. Musical instruments appear from trunks and sea bags and hiking packs. Such a diversity! One would think the music would be bedlam, but no, not entirely. Recently my mother taught us all a hundred and three verses of "Lucy is a Dandy in the Bushes but She has Legs like Sticks," and after she had sung all she knew, the others remembered another forty-odd verses. My father went to bed early that evening, and Melanchthon carved a small duck from a piece of firewood.

It is one of the miracles of my house that these rag-tags can produce harmony. It won't last; I know it won't. Each newcomer with an instrument frightens me; here comes our destroyer, I think. But no, our destroyer has not yet come.

And truly, there is no room for another here. I'd be in trouble if anyone I invited ever came. I can believe that there are already sixty-five only by counting them as they leave each morning to forage for their contributions to the soup. It is not possible. I compared the area of the house with the area of a person lying down multiplied by sixty-five; it is not possible. But there they go, out the door with their foraging implements: knives, hooks, nets, ropes, a Bible, a can of Dog-Away by which we snatch choice bones, and a ragged five-dollar bill. Sixty-three, sixty-four, sixty-five.

Where do they sleep? It might be possible if they stood up, but I look every night and no one is standing up.

Do they, at night, retire behind the closed doors that lead to strange places? These doors appear; I gather my courage and open them; they do not lead to the outside; they lead, instead, to shadowy rooms without floors, to passageways, to flights of stairs that double back, climbing up and up, for instance, while one pants for breath, only to open out again into the main room of the cottage.

My father does not remember building the house this way. I have mentioned the stairways and the rooms without floors to him and he denies all knowledge of them. My mother acts frightened when I question her. "Don't talk about things like that," she says. Neither of my parents wonders where the sixty-five people sleep. "Let them stay awake," says my father. "That's right," says my mother. For once she agrees with him.

For the moment I am not worried. They can sleep in the rooms without floors if they find comfort there. But I must do something before my child comes. I hear babies crying in the secret rooms, my milk comes in, I search and find nothing. Those doors must be boarded up, the rooms floored, or a father found to help me watch over this child.

The next day I asked Melanchthon. "What do you think is the proper job of a father?"

He looked startled. "Why ask me?" he said.

Now I was startled. "You have five children."

"That's true," he said, "but I do not think of myself as a father. I'm a wood carver. That is my talent. My wife has always said I was a zero as a father. She raises the children. She takes great pride in doing everything right, so I let her do everything. It would be too bad to have things done wrong."

"Then why does she need us to send soup?"

"She doesn't. She just wants me to provide it," he answered.

It was a long time before I had finished thinking about that and was ready to talk again. Melanchthon had taken up a fine chisel and his mallet and was outlining a curve in a huge fire log I had been saving for a winter celebration. A duck was being born under his hands.

I decided to risk being candid. "I think one of the proper jobs of fatherhood is taking the responsibility for a particular child, even if there are others to share in his instruction. A mother alone is not strong enough to protect the child from the evils of the world," I said. "Even a wood carver could help."

He broke in. "What evils do you mean?"

"The primary evil is the disappearance," I answered. "I have given birth before, but each time the baby has soon vanished. All that is left is crying from the inner rooms. No one has done anything; no one knows anything. My mother binds my breasts and I become bitter."

"Is that all?" he asked. "Don't you want any more from a man that that?"

"I don't know," I answered. "I haven't thought about it." I tried to make the matter more objective to appeal to his masculinity. "The big problem is the disappearance, which, if widespread, would lead to a world without children, or play, or art, or truth." I could see that I was getting more grandiose than universal so I dropped it and went on to the main issue. "If you could keep my child from disappearing…" I had brought up the question; now I waited for his response.

He chiseled out a bit of soft wood, leaving a curve like that of a feather. He walked around to the other side and looked for other places to make beginnings. It was a large log, much too large to use for a duck, but I did not mention it.

I continued to wait, though questions came to me and I wanted to ask them. I wanted him to answer quickly, yes, and then my mind would be free to go on. But I waited, quiet, while apple wood shavings like soft under-feathers drifted to the fire on the up-draft.

Then with a smile he spoke. "You're not direct, little one, but you're open." He went on. "We'd have to get rid of the old folks," he said, still working with the duck, making quick, light motions that sent chips and shavings cascading to the hearth, an occasional sliver floating toward the fire.

I was silent. Where could they go? This was their home. I couldn't do it, I thought.

I went to the fire to stir the soup, not daring to ask another question. The conversation was over with me no more secure than before and his presence just as tenuous.

When Melanchthon came back from his foraging for the day, I said, lowering my voice so the others couldn't hear, "I don't know how to get rid of the old folks."

"Are you sure that's what you want?" he asked.

I was sure. I'd thought it over. I wanted my child.

That evening he built a fire of many sticks. After a time the coals burned red under the pile of logs. The logs he had brought in were heavy, soaked with water from the January thaw, and those already in the fire cracked and sizzled.

When the music began, he called to my mother. "Come sing to us, old lady," he said, and smiled his elfin smile.

"Mother, you're tired," I said, my resolution wavering. "Why don't you turn in early tonight instead of wearing yourself out singing?"

She ignored me and yielded to the persuasion of white, pointed teeth against a frame of pointed, black beard.

"What happened to my true love," she sang, "who in my younger days surrounded me with tidbits from Olympus," her voice rising with conviction. "Who later on forgot my beauty and my wisdom, thinking only of his gifts and worth." Verse after verse she sang, up the octave by half steps, while my father stood by the hearth talking loudly of his exertions and her failures. He told of building the cottage with carefully fitted, uncut stones from all his travels, brought by his own power to this site, all for my mother who wasted her time singing the old songs handed down from her people, and never swept the hearth he had built her with such pain to his back, lifting each heavy stone. He told about the spider-web window he had pieced together (it was for her, he said) and his torn fingers from the bits of stained glass arranged to change scenes as the sun rose and set and with the tides and the solstices, and she never even washed his fine window. He told of his accuracy in directing each day by reading the window and how she countermanded his orders and went behind his back, singing, and never caring for his gifts and worth. As she sang higher, his voice became more frantic, "She let moss grow in the cracks!" His head bobbed up and down as he spoke with gnarled rage and white hair stringing down his chest, and she sang on, "Tell me, Pa, why your true love left you," and he talked louder and louder, until there was no song and no story, only the clanging of his lid of righteousness against her kettle of conviction, and then she was singing as high as her voice would go, more and more spiteful, "She left you since you care no longer for her soup and singing, only for your glass and stones," in such a voice that was all but unbearable, until he swung up a wetted log, with the same strength that he as a young man had used to build the stone hearth, and threw the log that quieted her at last, while he himself fell to the stones with a black face and his story told.

We buried them the next day, deep under the melting snow. The window was washed and read every half hour, culminating with the graveside reading brought by message brigade from the cottage.

All this might well have brought my child early, but no, there was only the usual kicking in my belly. The household went on much as before, except that we drew lots for the privilege of reading the window aloud each morning and the daily soup was no longer called "soup du jour" out of respect for my mother's euphemisms. We called it "garbage soup from Tenth and Main" or "garbage soup with leek and lentil," depending on the predominant taste, by common consent.

But he will arrive soon. I am heavy and my belly needs a wheelbarrow to carry it around. I stand against tables to rest my load; I read lying down with the book perched on the kicking baby. I read the magazines that tell how to get a man to stay and be the father. Melanchthon tells me to stop trying to please everyone and learn to please myself, but I am desperate – to please myself I have to find a father for my child. He says to relax, that if I please myself I'll attract the kind of father I'm looking for, but if I try to please everyone, I'll be so commonplace I'll only attract the mediocre. He's right, I know he's right, but there isn't time to follow his advice. Instead, I have bought the products that the magazines recommend. Now that my mother is gone I can work on this aspect instead of spending all my time on the soup. She used to tell me that the soup would catch and hold a man. Everyone has advice but none of it works.

The magazines have an entirely different story. Use the products, they say, and be beautiful. I use four products on my hair, nine on my face, deodorant sprays and skin-softening creams on every part of my body.

And I am following the tips for being uninhibited and spontaneous, like tickling myself with a feather, and looking a different direction after I blink than I was before – that's "flirting," they say. Of course, I cannot be completely uninhibited because of my shape. As my belly grows larger, the rest of me gets thinner, and I can't keep my balance. But I lie on the bed (I inherited the bedroom) and read the magazines and tickle myself with a feather and practice being uninhibited.

It all has an effect, though not the one I'd hoped for: the process server becomes more attentive each day. He has made arrangements with a doctor who will deliver my child. He ladles out the soup evenings, saying that I shouldn't be on my feet so long. He says he likes the effect of my new beauty program and brings me ads and coupons, once even bringing me a bottle of a rare emollient to rub into my belly so that there will not be stretch marks. I rub, but the stretch marks are already there from all the lost children.

Melanchthon does not notice my beauty program. He carves and chisels for hours each day and covers his work when he is gone. "The unveiling of this duck," he says, "will coincide with the birth of the new child." How he's going to time his art to coincide with nature I don't know, but he seems quite sure of himself. My show will be stolen, no doubt, by his; my child will squall and fill his pants while Melanchthon's admirable duck will remain quiet and perfect.

And now I feel the beginnings. In the middle of a breath, the breath stops – a pain comes to my back and courses around me like a tighter and tighter girdle. I lie on the cot under the spider-web window, as it is proper to do during childbirth, and read the scenes which change with each pain. Endlessly fascinating, the window occupies me, shortening the times between the roller-coaster of pain.

The doctor has come, thanks to the process server. I have been prepared. The doctor sits beside me and asks questions. I lie with my eyes closed answering him. He writes the answers on a magic slate, then lifts the plastic film, erasing them. I refuse drugs.

"Have you ever had tuberculosis?"

"Multiple sclerosis?"

"Elephantiasis?"

"Syphilis or other venereal disease?"

"Psychosis?"

My child is coming and I bite my tongue, screaming at the doctor deep in my throat. It feels good. I scream again, noiselessly, and bloody my tongue.

He records my answers on the magic slate.

"Have you ever been convicted of a felony?"

"A larceny?"

"A buggery?"

"A malicious intent?"

Between my legs the birthing hole gapes wide like the yawn one can't control. My child presses. The rim widens.

"Have you ever worked in macramé?"

"Fenced epeé?"

"Done batik in your spare time?"

"Put the shot?"

"If not, why not?"

He wipes the wetness from my chin. I seize his wrist in my teeth, glad to bloody him and not myself. "Why are you asking me these questions?" I ask, behind the mouthful of wrist.

"Let go," he says sharply. "We have to determine whether or not you are fit to be a mother." He takes up the magic slate again.

This time there is no stopper to my scream as I push the child out toward the world. No tongue, no wrist, just a scream. I scare myself. It can't really be that bad. I scream again, to scare the doctor.

"Did you wear clothes for decoration or for cover?"

"Did you masturbate with objects or play doctor with your brother?"

"Which would you rather kill, your mother or your father?"

I push again, hard, and my child erupts in desperation, breaking the rim of the birthing hole, a tearing of myself, such a numbing, and the first orgasm since the night in Melanchthon's hammock.

"Both of them!" I scream. There is a stirring nearby and I, with my eyes tight closed, say in a normal tone, "Isn't anyone going to help me?"

Hands wipe me off and I feel the hot, sticky baby lying on my caved-in belly. "You don't need any help. The baby's born." It is Melanchthon's voice. I open my eyes.

"Have you a statement for the magic slate?" the doctor asks. "This is the supreme experience in a woman's life." His stylus is poised over the plastic. "Tell us all about it."

"Am I fit to be a mother?"

The doctor writes vigorously. "I'll let you know later," he says.

Melanchthon lifts the baby off my belly. I hear a slap and a baby wail before I fall asleep, so tired, so very tired.

I missed the soup that evening but when the singing began, I woke up. Melanchthon's hammock was gone from the beams over the hearth, his carving tools were not in their niche. I was afraid to look for my child. My breasts were tight and I needed to nurse, but I was afraid to look.

The process server sat beside the cot. He spoke to me. "You have a fine, healthy baby," he said. "Congratulations and best wishes," he continued, "and many happy returns."

How was it possible, with no proper father?

"Look here," said the process server. "Right here."

I looked, finally, and beside the cot was my child, asleep in a hollow carved between wings that arched, promising flight. The process server rocked the baby, pushing webbed rockers with his toe.

/\/\/\/\/\

About the Author

Marcia Lewton, using the name Marcia Blumenthal, has published stories and poems in many literary magazines and collections and is the author of *Central Ink: A Soul's Quest Through Dream Work and Art*, published by Trafford Press, and a poetry chapbook, *In the Heart of Town, Still Digging*, published by Barnwood Press.

Marcia Lewton lives in Port Townsend, Washington, on the Olympic Peninsula.

ISBN 1-41200987-1